Jilly Cooper is a well-known journalist, writer and media superstar. The author of many number one bestselling novels, including *Riders*, *Rivals*, *Polo*, *The Man Who Made Husbands Jealous*, *Appassionata*, *Score!* and *Pandora*, she and her husband live in Gloucestershire.

Jilly Cooper was appointed OBE in the 2004 Queen's Birthday Honours List.

By Jilly Cooper

FICTION
Pandora

The Rutshire Chronicles:
Riders
Rivals
Polo
The Man Who Made Husbands Jealous
Appassionata
Score!

NON-FICTION
Animals in War
Class
How to Survive Christmas
Hotfoot to Zabriskie Point (with Patrick Lichfield)
Intelligent and Loyal
Jolly Marsupial
Jolly Super
Jolly Superlative
Jolly Super Too
Super Cooper
Super Jilly
Super Men and Super Women
The Common Years
Turn Right at the Spotted Dog
Work and Wedlock
Angels Rush In
Araminta's Wedding

CHILDREN'S BOOKS
Little Mabel
Little Mabel's Great Escape
Little Mabel Saves the Day
Little Mabel Wins

ROMANCE
Bella
Emily
Harriet
Imogen
Lisa and Co
Octavia
Prudence

ANTHOLOGIES
The British in Love
Violets and Vinegar

EMILY

Jilly Cooper

CORGI BOOKS

EMILY
A CORGI BOOK : 0 552 15249 8

Originally published in Great Britain by
Arlington Books Ltd

PRINTING HISTORY
Arlington Books edition published 1975
Corgi edition published 1976
Corgi edition reissued 2005

1 3 5 7 9 10 8 6 4 2

Set in 11/14pt Times by
Kestrel Data, Exeter, Devon.

Corgi Books are published by Transworld Publishers,
61–63 Uxbridge Road, London W5 5SA,
a division of The Random House Group Ltd,
in Australia by Random House Australia (Pty) Ltd,
20 Alfred Street, Milsons Point, Sydney, NSW 2061, Australia,
in New Zealand by Random House New Zealand Ltd,
18 Poland Road, Glenfield, Auckland 10, New Zealand
and in South Africa by Random House (Pty) Ltd,
Endulini, 5a Jubilee Road, Parktown 2193, South Africa.

Printed and bound in Great Britain by
Cox & Wyman Ltd, Reading, Berkshire.

Papers used by Transworld Publishers are natural, recyclable
products made from wood grown in sustainable forests.
The manufacturing processes conform to the environmental
regulations of the country of origin.

To Claire
with love

Author's Note

The idea for Emily first came to me in 1969. I wrote it as a long short story called CIRCLES, and it appeared in serial form in *19*. I took the story and completely re-wrote it, and the result is EMILY.

EMILY

Chapter One

If Nina hadn't bugged me, I'd never have gone to Annie Richmond's party.

'Cedric is beginning to take you for granted,' she said, hurling clothes into a weekend case.

'Cedric,' I said crossly, 'is getting his career together. As soon as he's adopted as a candidate, we'll get married.'

'Because it's better for candidates to have wives,' said Nina. 'He shouldn't leave you alone so much. Your first weekend back from holiday, looking a million and a half dollars – anyone else wouldn't be able to keep his hands off you – but old Seedcake just swans off to another political rally.'

'I'm very happy about my relationship with Cedric. And that's mine,' I snapped, removing a yellow shirt she was surreptitiously packing in one corner of her case. 'Cedric keeps me on the straight and narrow,' I went on.

'He's turned you into a bore,' said Nina. 'You used to be lovely company when you were playing fast and loose with half of London.'

'I want a sense of purpose in my life,' I protested. 'I don't want to die in Chelsea with my knickers down.'

Nina went to the mirror and started slapping Man-tan all over her face.

'Where are you off to?' I said.

'Home. I don't want my mother fussing about me looking washed out – and tomorrow I'm going out with an amazingly dishy new man. Now aren't you jealous?'

'No,' I lied. 'You just give up certain things when you're engaged.'

'Like fun. Just because Seedcake's put a ring on your finger, he thinks he's entitled to neglect you all the time. I think you ought to go to Annie Richmond's orgy; she's got this fantastically good-looking cousin coming. If he gave you a whirl, you'd soon forget about Seedcake.'

'Don't call him that,' I stormed. 'Anyway, I've nothing in common with Annie Richmond's friends any more.'

Nina laughed meaningly. 'You mean Cedric hasn't. She reminds him of your past and that come-hither look your eyes had once. You're scared of going because you think you might fancy some-one. If you were really hooked on Seedcake, you wouldn't be frightened to go.'

I felt depressed after she'd gone. I'd done all the boring things like washing my hair, shaving my legs and doing my nails yesterday, in the hope that I might see Cedric tonight. After a few minutes moping I settled down to half-heartedly cleaning the flat, then washing the suntan-oil out of a few shirts.

I looked at Cedric's photograph beside my bed, thought how good-looking he was, then I read a book on Conservative policy. It was incredibly boring and nearly sent me to sleep. Cedric telephoned – as he said he would – on the dot of ten o'clock.

'How heavenly to hear you, darling,' I said, overwhelmed with love. 'How are you?'

'Oh, full of beans,' he said in his hooray, political voice, which meant there were people in the room. As he told me what a success the meeting had been and how well his speech had gone, I examined the diamond and sapphire ring he'd given me.

Finally he said, 'What are you going to do with yourself all weekend?'

'Annie Richmond's throwing an orgy,' I said lightly. 'As you're not here, I was thinking of going.'

Cedric laughed heartily and disbelievingly. 'I thought you'd grown out of that sort of party,' he said. 'I must go darling. I'll ring you on Monday and we'll have dinner. Take care of yourself; and remember, no orgies. They're bad for my reputation.'

I put the telephone down feeling extremely irritated. What was the point of spending ten days alone in the South of France – Cedric naturally couldn't get away – boring myself silly getting a suntan for his sake, when he wasn't around to appreciate it?

I looked out at the September evening – the dusk with its suggestion of autumn and nights drawing in and another year passing shot waves of repressed lust through me. I thought of sex and sin and all the men in the world I'd never have the chance to get my hands on now.

It was such a long, long time since I'd been to a good party. Cedric thought all my friends so frivolous and idiotic, he'd scared them away.

I looked at his photograph again – short, fair hair, clear, blue eyes, a determined chin.

'Life is earnest, life is real,' I said to myself firmly. 'Cedric would hate me to go to Annie Richmond's orgy, so I won't go.'

An hour later, feeling horribly guilty, I crept up the stairs to Annie Richmond's flat, having heard the roar of the party all the way down the street. Annie opened the door.

'Emily,' she cried joyfully, giving me a huge hug. 'I never dreamed you'd come.'

She was wearing a dress so cut out there was hardly any of it left. I was wearing a backless black dress, pretty low at the front and welded together with safety pins, as usual, which I'd never dared show Cedric. I'd put on weight since I last wore it and was falling out all over the place. I just hoped I looked a bit like Sophia Loren.

Annie looked at me with approval. 'Stripped for action, that's more like the old Emily,' she said, handing me a glass.

'I've only just popped in for a quick drink,' I said. 'Cedric's away.'

'I know,' she smiled knowingly. 'There's lots of talent in there, so go in and forage for yourself.'

The next room was impossibly, clamorously full of good-looking people trying to shout each other down. I felt very nervous, so I drank my disgusting drink straight down, and quickly had another. I didn't know a soul, but then Annie turned over her friends so fast.

A handsome Australian in a red shirt came over and started to chat me up. His eyes smouldered under bushy black eyebrows.

I knew that look of old: I feel I know every inch of you already, so let's get on with it – it stated un-equivocally.

'Bloody awful row,' he said. 'Pity I can't lip-read.' He gazed at my mouth and then at my black dress, which was descending fast. Any minute I'd be top-less. I heaved it up. 'Leave it,' he said. 'I'm enjoying the view.'

He was clearly a superstud, and would have whipped me down the passage and under Annie's duvet in two seconds flat. But I wanted to stay upright, not flat. Suppressing the waves of lust that were sweeping over me, I started to shout at him about Cedric and his political career. He can't have heard much of what I was saying, but seemed to get the message and drifted off.

I was then collared by an ancient or more an elderly Wren, a model with long red hair and skinny white hands, who went on and on about her split ends.

Suddenly there was a commotion by the door.

'But Annie,' said a man's voice, 'I thought I was coming to an orgy. Where are the wall-to-wall couples? The lovely girls in tiger skins?'

Split Ends caught her breath. I, like everyone else, turned around. My jaw clanged – for standing in the doorway was one of the most sensationally attractive men I had ever seen. He was tall, with broadish shoulders, long black hair, restless dark eyes with a wicked gleam in them, and an arrogant sulky mouth. He oozed sexuality. He looked round the room, as cool and haughty as a prince, yet he had an explosive quality – I've come out of the jungle and no-one's going to tame me, he seemed to say. Every woman in the room was going mad with desire; me included. The only problem was a very beautiful dark girl dressed in what looked like a bikini entirely made of flowers, who was hanging possessively on his arm.

'You promised me an orgy, Annie,' he said, coldly. 'All I can see here is a deb's tea-party.'

Annie Richmond took him and the dark girl by the arm and hustled them towards the bar.

'It'll start warming up soon,' I could hear her

saying. 'There's a lot of fun people coming later.'

I noticed she gave him a whole bottle of whisky to himself, while the rest of us had to make do with the revolting cough mixture.

Gradually the conversation started to soar and dip again. 'Who's that?' everyone was asking.

I turned to Split Ends. 'Who's that?' I said.

She looked at me incredulously. 'You mean to say you don't know?'

A stockbroker with a pink face whose eyes were about level with my cleavage, came past and filled up our glasses.

'That's Rory Balniel,' he said. 'He's a bit of a menace.'

'He's Annie's cousin,' said Split Ends, watering at the mouth, 'and quite the most evil man in London.'

'In what way?' I asked.

'Oh, getting drunk and breaking people's hearts deliberately. Everything you can think of, and a lot more besides.'

'He looks like the leader of a Cossack horde,' I said. 'What nationality is he?'

'Scottish, with foreign, I think French, on one side. His family own masses of land in the Highlands, but all the money's tied up in trusts, and he can't get his hands on it. He's been sent down from everywhere imaginable. He hit London about a month ago. I don't think he's been sober since.'

'He's a bit of a menace,' repeated the stockbroker, looking longingly at my cleavage.

19

'He's supposed to be a very good painter,' said Split Ends.

'The only thing he's been painting recently is the town red,' said the stockbroker.

'He treats women appallingly,' said Split Ends.

'Has he treated you appallingly?' I asked.

'Not yet,' she said with a sigh, 'but I'm working on it.'

I looked around again. Rory Balniel was leaning against the mantelpiece. Two girls who looked as though the head groom had been polishing and curry-combing them for weeks, so sleek and patently glossy were they, were vying for his attention.

He filled up their glasses from the whisky bottle, then suddenly, he lifted his head, yawned slightly and looked in my direction. I shot him a glance I hadn't used in months. One of pure naked come-hithering sex. It didn't work. He looked away without interest.

'Hard luck,' said Split Ends, avidly drinking in this classic case of indifference at first sight. 'You're obviously not his type.'

'He's probably queer,' I said crossly. 'Most Don Juans are latent homosexuals anyway.'

Split Ends looked at me pityingly, then grabbed a plate of food from a nearby table.

'I'm going to offer him a stuffed date,' she said with a giggle, and wheeled across the room towards him.

I turned my back and talked to the stockbroker. It

was a calculated gesture. If anything was likely to turn Rory Balniel on, it was my back – brown, smooth and bare from the nape of my neck almost to the base of my spinal column, unmarred by any bikini marks.

I imagined his dark, restless eyes ranging over me and thinking, 'That's the sort of girl who sunbathes without a bikini top. Mettlesome, ready for anything, even being treated appallingly by Rory Balniel.'

But when I looked around, he was talking to Split Ends, and was still hemmed in by the masses.

Sexless beast, I decided; or perhaps it's my sex appeal that's slipping.

Cedric was right. These people were frivolous and uninteresting. The evening wore on. People were dancing in the next room, drinking a lot and necking a little. No-one was actually orgying. I kept making up my mind to go home, but some instinctive lack of self-preservation made me stay. I felt jolted, uneasy and horribly aware of Rory Balniel. There was an unconscious glitter about him, a sinister stillness that set him apart from everyone else. One had to admit his force.

Split Ends and the girl he'd arrived with, who I discovered was called Tiffany (I bet she made it up), were still trying to engage his attention. He was laughing a lot at their jokes, but a little late on cue. As he filled his glass, his hand was quite steady. Only the glint in his eyes betrayed how much he'd drunk.

Annie Richmond went up to him and removed the bottle of whisky, 'Rory, love, I don't mean to nag.'

'Women always say that when they're about to nag,' he said, taking the whisky back from her.

People were really getting uncorked now. Couples had disappeared into other rooms, a beautiful African girl was dancing by herself. A fat man was telling filthy stories to an ugly American girl who had passed out on the floor. The Australian in the red shirt, who had chatted me up earlier, turned out to be Split Ends' boyfriend. He was not pleased at her paying so much attention to Rory Balniel and came strutting into the room wearing a Mickey Mouse mask, expecting everyone to laugh.

'Where did you get that mask?' said Rory Balniel.

'Annie gave it to me.'

'You should wear it all the time. Every day. Always. To the office. It suits you. Gives your face a distinction it didn't have before.'

'Don't be stupid,' said the Australian furiously, wrenching off the mask. He nearly tripped over the ugly American girl who was now snoring on the floor.

'Jesus Christ, why doesn't somebody move her?'

'She's quite happy,' said Rory Balniel. 'I expect she needs sleep. Anyway, she gives the room a lived-in feeling.'

'Someone might tread on her face,' said the Australian, lugging her out of the way.

'Good thing, too. It could only improve things,' said Rory Balniel. He was trying to balance a glass on one of his fingers, managing to look like a Siamese cat. Inevitably, the glass crashed to the floor.

Split Ends and Tiffany howled with laughter. A blonde, attracted by the tinkle of broken glass, came over and joined the group.

'I hear you paint,' she said, 'I'd love to sit for you sometime.'

Rory Balniel looked her over. 'But would you lie for me later, darling? That's the point.'

He started to undo the buttons of Split Ends' dress.

'I say,' said the pink-faced stockbroker. 'You can't do that here. Unfair to Annie. Know what I mean?'

'No,' said Rory Balniel unpleasantly.

He had now undone all Split Ends' buttons to reveal a very dirty bra.

'Don't,' she said crossly, trying to do them up again.

His dark face set into a mask of malice. 'If you throw yourself open to the public, sweetheart, you must expect people to want to see over you.'

Split Ends flounced off.

'Good riddance,' said the blonde, snuggling up to him.

'She's a silly cow,' he said unemotionally, draining his drink.

'What did you say?' said the Australian, who was still smarting under the crack about the Mickey Mouse mask. 'Are you referring to my girlfriend?'

'I was referring to the silly cow,' said Rory. 'And if she's your girlfriend, she's even stupider than she looks. And don't come on all macho with me, you bloody colonial, or I'll kick you back down under, where you belong.' Picking up a wine bottle, he deliberately cracked it on the edge of the mantel-piece and brandished the jagged end in the Australian's face.

The Australian clenched his fists. 'I'll call the police,' he said, half-heartedly.

'*What* are you going to call the police?' said Rory Balniel.

He picked up another glass from the mantelpiece, and smashed it on the floor.

The Australian puffed out his cheeks, and then beat a hasty retreat.

The two girls roared with laughter again, enjoying themselves hugely. Then they looked around for the next distraction.

He's absolutely poisonous, I decided. How does anyone put up with him?

Picking his way disapprovingly over the broken pieces of glass, the little stockbroker came over and asked me to dance.

'I told you he was a menace, did I not?' he asked in an undertone.

He then proceeded to make the most ferocious

passes at me on the dance floor. I can never understand why little men are so lecherous. I suppose it's
more concentrated. Fortunately, one of my safety
pins gave way and plunged into him, which cooled
his ardour a bit. But two seconds later he was back
on the attack.

A quarter of an hour later, black and blue and as
mad as a wet cat, I returned to collect my bag. I was
really leaving this time. I found Rory Balniel was
sitting on the sofa – Tiffany and the blonde on either
side of him. Both girls were holding hands with each
other across him, but were so tight, neither of them
realized it.

'Rory, darling,' whispered the blonde.

'Rory, angel,' murmured Tiffany.

It looked so ridiculous I burst out laughing. He
looked up and started to laugh too.

'I think they're made for each other,' he said. And
extracting himself, got up and came over.

I leaned against the wall, partly because I was
slewed, partly because my legs wouldn't hold me up.
The impact of this man, close up, was absolutely
faint-making.

'Hullo,' he said.

'Hullo,' I said. I've always been a wizard at
repartee.

He looked me over consideringly as if I was a
colour chart and he was selecting a shade.

'The drink has run out,' he said, taking a final slug
of whisky from the bottle.

He had very white, even teeth, but his fingers were quite heavily stained with nicotine.

'What did you say your name was?' he said. His voice had lost its earlier bitchy ring – it was soft and husky now.

'I didn't,' I said, 'but since you ask, it's Emily.'

'Emily – pretty name, old-fashioned name. Are you an old-fashioned girl?'

'Depends what you mean by old-fashioned – prunes and prisms Victorian or Nell Gwyn?'

He took my hand.

He's drunk, I said to myself firmly, trying not to faint with excitement.

'You're like a little Renoir,' he said.

'Are those the outsize ones, all grapes and rippling with flesh?' I said.

'No, that's Rubens. Renoirs are soft and blonde and blue-eyed, with pink flesh tones. It's funny,' he added, shooting me an Exocet look, 'you're not my type at all, but you excite the hell out of me.'

I looked down, and to my horror, saw that my fingers were coiling around his, and watched my only unbitten nail gouging into the centre of his palm.

Then suddenly I felt his fingers on my engagement ring.

I tried to jerk my hand away, but he held on to it, and examined the ring carefully.

'Who gave that to you?' he said.

'Cedric,' I said. 'My – er – fiancé. It's a terrible

word, isn't it?' I gave a miserable, insincere little giggle.

'It's a terrible ring, too,' he said.

'It cost a lot of money,' I said defensively.

'Why isn't he here?'

I explained about Cedric being in Norfolk and furthering his political career.

'How long have you been engaged?'

'Nearly eighteen months.'

The smile Rory Balniel gave me wasn't at all pleasant. 'Does he make love on all four channels?' he said.

I tried, but failed, to look affronted. 'He doesn't make love to me much at all,' I muttered.

Rory Balniel was swinging the empty whisky bottle between finger and thumb.

'He doesn't care about you at all, does he?'

'Cedric and I have a good thing going.'

'If you're mad about a girl, you don't let her out of your sight.'

Instinctively my eyes slid to Tiffany, who was now sleeping peacefully, her head on the blonde girl's shoulder.

'I'm not exactly mad about her,' he said.

'She's stunning looking,' I said, wistfully.

He shrugged his shoulders.

'Rolls-Royce body maybe, but a Purley mind.'

I giggled again. Suddenly he bent his head and kissed my bare shoulder. I could feel the ripples of excitement all the way down to my toes. Any moment my dress, safety pins and all, was going to burst into flames. I could have died with excitement.

I took a deep breath. 'I've got a bottle of whisky at home,' I said.

'Well, let's go then,' he said.

Chapter Two

I wasn't proud of my behaviour. I knew I was treating Cedric abominably, but then I'd never before in my life encountered such a personification of temptation as Rory Balniel. And, like Oscar Wilde, I've always been able to resist anything except temptation.

We wandered along the King's Road, trying to find a taxi, and giggling a great deal as we tried out all the baths sitting outside the bath shop. Then we passed an art gallery. Rory peered moodily through the window at the paintings.

'Look at that crap,' he said. 'There but for the gracelessness of God go I, the greatest genius of the twentieth century – which reminds me, I've got to see a man about my painting at eleven tomorrow. You'd better set your alarm clock when we get home.'

Presumptuous, I thought. Does he think I'll succumb so easily?

Rory suddenly saw a taxi and flagged it down. We kissed all the way home.

29

God – I was enjoying myself. I'd never felt a millionth of that raging, abandoned glory, the whole time I'd known Cedric. As the taxi chugged along, and the orange numbers on the meter rocketed relentlessly upwards, so did my temperature. Rory had such a marvellously lean, broad-shouldered body. It must have been something to do with both being an artist and having Gallic blood, but he was certainly an artist at French kissing.

All the same, somewhere inside me, an insistent voice was warning me to call a halt. I was back-sliding at the speed of light, doing all the things I'd done before I'd met Cedric, giving in too quickly, losing too quickly and feeling just as insecure and unhappy as I'd been in the past. I'll say goodbye to him firmly at the door, I told myself. Then when we got to the door I thought: I'll just give him a very quick drink to be sociable and then out he goes.

No sooner had we entered the flat and I'd given him some whisky, than I rushed off to the bathroom, cleaned my teeth and emptied half a bottle of Nina's scent over myself. I then went and removed the Georgette Heyer novel from my bedside table and replaced it with a couple of intellectual French novels.

I went into the drawing-room.

'Where did you learn to pour drinks like this one?' he asked.

'I once worked in a bar,' I replied.

'This is a septuple,' said Rory, draining the glass.

'I'm seeing septuple,' I said. 'After all the booze I've shipped, I can see at least seven of you at the moment. A magnificent seven, admittedly.'

'Then we can have a gang-bang,' said Rory with a whoop. 'Annie's orgy is going to materialize after all.'

Primly, I sat down on the sofa. He sat beside me.

'Well? Orgy on?' he asked, staring at me, but making no move.

I hunted around nervously for something to say.

'Keep still,' he said. 'You've got something in your hair.'

I never knew if I had or I hadn't. But he removed whatever it was and then, unsmilingly, he came closer and kissed me.

After a while, I had a pang of conscience and tried to push him away. 'I'll make some coffee,' I muttered. 'Really, I am engaged to Cedric and he wouldn't approve at all.'

'Shut up,' he said gently. Very slowly, he undid all the safety pins holding my dress together – first the one joining the bodice and shoulder-strap, then the little gold pin just below the zip top, and finally the two securing my strapless bra.

Naked to the waist now, I still couldn't move.

'Little Renoir,' he said softly.

Stop! I said to myself, but I couldn't move.

It was morning when I woke. I hadn't closed the curtains properly, so the sun seared straight into my eyes like a laser beam. Even more searing was

31

Cedric's smile – his photograph stared right at me. Frantic with thirst, I reached for the glass by the bed, gulped at it, and nearly threw up. It was whisky.

Inching my hand to the right, I practically went through the ceiling as I encountered a body. Cedric's. I gave a groan. Cedric was in Norfolk, rallying the faithful. The unfaithful was lying in my bed. I drew back the covers to look at the man beside me. One glance told me I had impeccable taste when I was drunk. And total lack of judgement too, by allowing myself to get laid on the first date.

Slowly piecing the evening together, I looked at the clock. Half past ten. I was supposed to wake him up to see a man about some paintings. I got up and washed. My face looked all blotchy, like garlic sausage, so I slapped on some casual-looking make-up. Then I threw a handful of Alka-Seltzers into a glass of water, waited until the froth subsided, drank it down and went back to bed.

I think Rory was still drunk when I woke him up. He got up, drew the curtains, and then groped for a cigarette.

'What happened last night?'

'Oh, Rory,' I wailed. 'Don't you remember anything?'

'Well, I remember spending a rain-soaked childhood among the sheep in Scotland, and being sacked from Harrow and being sent down from

Oxford. I remember coming to London to sell some paintings. After that I think the drink took over. Then there seems to have been a lot of parties.'

'We were at Annie Richmond's party,' I said.

'So we were.'

'And we both had quite a bit to drink and then we came back here.'

'Well, well, well,' he said, getting into the crumpled bed. 'And did we?'

'Oh, God! Can't you remember that?'

'Was I . . . er . . . did I perform adequately?' He didn't seem embarrassed, only curious.

'You were absolutely sensational, that's what makes it so awful,' I said and, rolling over, I buried my face in the pillow and burst into tears.

He stroked my hair, but I went on sobbing. 'I'm not usually like this. I don't just pick up men at parties and leap into bed with them on the first night. At least, not recently,' I wailed. 'And you'd better step on it, you've got to see that man about your paintings at eleven o'clock.'

'So I have.' Slowly he clambered out of bed and started to get dressed. I was shot through with misery, but I tried to make a joke of the situation.

'Don't think I've enjoyed meeting you, because I haven't,' I said with a deliberate sniff.

He laughed, and when he had dressed and cut himself shaving on Nina's pink plastic razor, he came back into the bedroom and said, 'You'll remember exactly what happened last night, won't you? When I write my memoirs, I'll need to pick your brains.'

I pulled a pillow over my head. 'There aren't any to pick,' I groaned.

'See you,' he said. Then he was gone.

I went through every kind of hell wondering if he'd come back. I castigated myself for the insanity of going to Annie Richmond's party, for letting Rory make love to me – which, despite his not remembering anything about it, had been an utterly intoxicating experience which would spoil me for Cedric for evermore.

The telephone rang three times, each time for Nina, and each time the caller got his head bitten off for not being Rory. At four o'clock, realizing he wasn't coming back, I got up, had a bath, cried for an hour and then poured myself a large whisky. Really, I was acquiring a lot of bad habits. I'd be eating between meals soon!

At six o'clock the doorbell rang. Keep calm, I told myself. Play it cool. It's bound to be the milkman, or some Salvation Army lady after loot.

But it was Rory, swaying in the doorway and looking green. 'I've just been sick in a dustbin,' he said.

I laughed, trying to keep the joy out of my face. 'Come in,' I said.

He headed straight for the whisky. 'May I have a drink?' he said. 'My hangover ought to go down in medical history. Childbirth has nothing on it.'

He had the most awful shakes.

'There's a reason for all this drinking,' he went on. 'But at the moment, I'm glad to say, I can't remember what it is. I really oughtn't to have come back – I'm afraid I've run out of money.'

'I've always wanted to keep a man,' I said. 'Stick with me, baby, and you'll be up to your ears in race-horses.'

'It's not as bad as that. I got on well at the art gallery.'

'Did he like your paintings?' I said.

He nodded. 'He's going to give me an exhibition in the spring.'

'But that's wonderful,' I said. 'You'll be famous.'

'I know.' He peered in the mirror, pushing a lock of black hair out of his eyes. 'I don't think it suits me. I feel terrible.'

'You ought to eat something,' I said.

'You're admirable. I wish I had a mother that fussed over me like that.'

In fact he was very ill all night and most of the next day; delirious and with a raging temperature, pouring with sweat, clinging to me, muttering incoherently and shaking like a puppy. On Sunday night, however, he felt better. Suddenly, picking up Cedric's photograph, he threw it out of the window.

'That wasn't very friendly,' I said, listening to the tinkle of broken glass.

'When's he coming back?'

'Tomorrow. Cedric's very good to me. He keeps

me on the rails. Before I met him, it was one lay-
about after another.'

The restless dark eyes travelled over me. 'That's
because you're a giver, Emily, and you hate hurting
people. You slept with all those men because you
couldn't say no rather than because you wanted to
say yes.'

'Oh, not always. Anyway, there weren't that many
of them – in single figures, that is.'

'If I rang you up and asked you out,' he went on,
undeterred, 'even if you didn't fancy me, you'd say
yes because you couldn't bear to upset me. Then
you'd send me a cable at the last moment, or get one
of your mates to ring up and say you were dying of
food poisoning.'

'How do you know?' I said sulkily.

'I know,' he said, and pulled me into his arms. The
waves of lust were rippling all over me again.

'You're ill,' I protested.

'Not that ill,' he said.

'I like sleeping with you,' he said, a couple of hours
later. 'Let's get married.'

I looked at him incredulously, reeling from the
shock.

'You'd better send Cedric a telegram immediately,' he said. 'I don't want him hanging around
being a bloody nuisance to us.'

'Did you say you wanted to marry me?' I whispered. 'You can't want to marry me. I mean, what

about all those girls after you? You could marry anyone. Why me?'

'I'm kinky that way,' he said. 'I'll try anything once.'

'But where will we live?' I said, bewildered.

'In Scotland. I've got a place up there. I'm much nicer in Scotland, London does frightful things to me – and I'm due to inherit a bit of money shortly, so we won't starve.'

'But . . . but . . .' I stammered. I really wanted him to take me in his arms and say he loved me to distraction, but then the telephone rang.

Rory picked it up. 'Hullo, who's that? Oh, Cedric.' A slightly malicious gleam came into his eyes. 'We haven't met. My name's Balniel, Rory Balniel. How was the political rally? Oh, well that's splendid. You deserve some compensation because I'm afraid Emily has just agreed to marry me – and she'll be dispensing with your disservices from now on.'

'Oh, no,' I protested. 'Poor Cedric.'

I could hear him spluttering away on the other end of the telephone.

'Well I'm afraid you've lost your deposit on this one,' said Rory, and put down the receiver.

'Cedric will be very, very angry,' I said in awe.

Chapter Three

Cedric wasn't the only one who was angry. Annie Richmond was livid, too.

'You can't marry Rory, he's never been faithful to anyone for more than five minutes. He's immoral and dreadfully spoilt. He even used to cheat at conkers when he was a little boy!'

Nina was even more discouraging. Genuine concern for me combined – when she'd actually met Rory in the flesh – with overwhelming envy.

'I know he's lovely to look at, but he's an absolute devil. You're batting out of your league. Cedric was far more suitable.'

'It was you in the first place,' I said crossly, 'who was so against Cedric, and hustled me off to Annie Richmond's party.'

'I never dreamed you'd go to these extremes. Where are you going to live?'

'In the Highlands, on an island. It sounds too romantic for words.'

Nina sighed. 'It is not romantic living on an island. What will you do, except talk to sheep and go mad while he slaps paint on canvases all day? You won't hold him in a million years. You'll be thoroughly miserable, and then come and snivel all over me. The only thing a whirl-wind courtship does is blow dust in everyone's eyes.'

I didn't care. I was hanging from chandeliers, swinging round lamp-posts. I was so deranged with love I didn't know what to do with myself. I felt I was drowning and I didn't want anyone to save me.

Another aspect that delighted me was the being married part of the whole thing. I'd never been cut out for a career and the thought that I could chuck in my nine-to-five job and spend the rest of my life looking after Rory filled me with joy. I had fantasies of greeting him at the door, after a hard day at his studio, a beautiful child hanging on each hand.

Three days later, Rory and I were married at Chelsea Register Office. I had been to see the Renoirs at the Tate, and wore a Laura Ashley dress and a black breton on the back of my head. Even Nina admitted I looked good.

Rory was waiting when we arrived, smoking and gazing moodily at the road. It was the first time I'd seen him in a suit – pale grey velvet with a black shirt.

'Isn't he the most beautiful thing you've ever seen!' I said rapturously.

'Yes,' said Nina. 'It isn't too late to change your mind.'

He smiled when he saw us, then his narrowed eyes fixed coldly on my hat. Tearing it from my head, he threw it on the ground and kicked it into the Kings Road, where a milk van ran over it.

'Don't you ever dare wear a hat again,' he said, ruffling my hair.

Then he took my hand and led me into the Register Office.

Afterwards we had a party and drank champagne, and flew to Paris for our honeymoon. When we arrived at our hotel – which was pretty, with shutters, vines and pink geraniums, overlooking the Seine – Rory ordered more champagne.

He was in a strange, wild mood. I wondered how much he'd drunk before he got to the Register Office. I very much wanted him to pounce on me and ravish me at once. I suddenly felt apprehensive, lost and very much alone.

I went off and had a bath. Isn't that what all brides do? All my things were new – sponge bag, flannel, talcum powder, toothbrush. Even my name was new – Emily Balniel.

I said it over and over to myself as I lay in the bath, with the water not too hot so I wouldn't emerge like a lobster.

I rubbed scented bath oil into every inch of my body and put on a new white negligée, fantastically expensive and pretty and virginal. I went into the bedroom, and waited for Rory's gasp of approval. It never came. He was on the telephone, his face ashen.

'Hullo,' he was saying. 'Hullo, yes, it's me all right. I know it's been a long time. Where am I? In Paris, at the Reconnaissance. Do you remember the Reconnaissance, darling? I just wanted to tell you that I got married this afternoon, so that makes us level again, doesn't it?' And, with a ghastly expression of triumph on his face, he dropped the telephone back in its cradle.

'Who were you ringing?' I asked.

He looked at me for a minute as though I were a stranger. There was the same sinister stillness, the lurking danger that I'd been so aware of the first night I met him.

'Who was it?' I asked again.

'Mind your own business,' he snarled. 'Just because I've married you, it doesn't give you the right to question all my movements.'

I felt as though he'd hit me. For a minute we stared at each other, bristling with hostility. Then he pulled himself together, apologized for jumping down my throat – and began to kiss me almost frenziedly.

When I woke up, in the middle of the night, I found him standing by the window, smoking a cigarette. He had his back to me but there was something infinitely despairing about the hunched set of his shoulders.

With a sick feeling of fear, I wondered why he had felt it necessary to ring up a woman on the first night of his honeymoon, and taunt her with the fact that he'd just got married.

Marriage, as I discovered on my honeymoon, may be a bed of roses, but there are plenty of thorns lying around.

Not that I found myself loving Rory any the less; rather the reverse, but he was not easy to live with. To begin with, I never knew what mood he was going to be in. There were the prolonged black glooms, followed by sudden firework bursts of affection, followed by an abstracted fit when he would sit for hours watching the sun on the plane trees outside our window. There were also the sudden, uncontrollable rages – in a smart French restaurant he had picked up a dish of potato purée, and hurled it at a passing fly!

I also had to get used to everyone looking at Rory rather than at me; and that was another thing about marriage. I couldn't spend hours tarting myself up to compete with all those svelte French women. If Rory suddenly decided he wanted to go out, it was straight out of bed, into the shower and 'what the hell do you want to bother with make-up for?'

I found being with him day in, day out, slightly claustrophobic. There wasn't a moment to shave my armpits or touch up the roots of my hair. He did quite a lot of work. I was longing for him to sketch me, and kept sweeping my hair back for him to admire the beauty of my bone structure, but he was far more interested in drawing old men and women with wrinkled faces in cafés. The drawings were amazingly good.

Chapter Four

We were sitting in bed one afternoon after one of those heavy French lunches, when suddenly there was a pounding on the door.

'Who the hell's that?' I asked.

'A chambermaid gone berserk and unable to contain herself,' said Rory, and shouted something very impolite in French.

The pounding went on.

'Perhaps it's the flics,' said Rory, getting out of bed and putting on his trousers. Through a haze of alcohol, I looked at his tousled black hair and broad brown shoulders.

Swearing, he unlocked the door. A beautiful woman stood there.

'Chérie,' she cried ecstatically. 'Bébé, I knew you were 'ere. The man on the desk was so discreet. He refuse to admit it.' And flinging her arms round Rory's neck, she kissed him on both cheeks.

'I think you are ver' unkind,' she went on reproachfully in a strong French accent, 'sloping off and getting married without a word to anyone. I mean, think of the wedding presents you missed.'

Rory looked half exasperated, half amused.

'I'm afraid this is my mother,' he said.

'Oh gosh,' I squeaked. 'How fright . . . I mean, how lovely. How do you do?'

It was a fine way to meet one's mother-in-law for the first time; sitting up in bed, wearing nothing but a crumpled sheet and a bright smile.

'This is Emily,' said Rory.

Rory's mother rushed across the room and hugged me.

'But you are so pretty,' she said. 'This pleases me very much. I keep telling Rory to find a nice wife and settle down. I know you will make 'im 'appy, and he will start behaving beautifully.'

'I'll try,' I faltered.

She was stunning looking – lush, opulent, exotic, with huge dark blue eyes, hair dyed the most terrific shade of strawberry blonde, the most marvellous legs and lots of jewellery. It was easy to see from where Rory got his traffic-stopping looks.

One of her eyelids was made up with brilliant violet eyeshadow, the other smeared with emerald green.

'I have just been to Dior for a fitting. I tried out their new make-up, it's a very pretty shade of green, no?'

'Where's Buster?' asked Rory.

'Coming later,' she said. 'He's having a drink with some friends.'

'He's lying,' said Rory. 'He couldn't possibly have a friend.'

Rory's mother giggled. 'Now, chérie, you must not be naughty. Buster is my second 'usband,' she explained to me. 'Rory's father, Hector, was my first.

'When I marry Buster, Rory say to me, "You're getting better at choosing husbands, maman, but not much."'

Rory's mother suddenly gave a shriek. 'Ah! *Mon Dieu,* I remember the taxi is still waiting downstairs. We 'ave run out of money. We knew you would have some, Rory, you're so rich now. Could you ring down and get the manager to pay the taxi?'

Rory looked at her with intense irritation, then he laughed, picked up the telephone and gabbled away in French.

'Ask 'im to send up some champagne,' said Rory's mother. 'At least two bottles, I want to drink my new daughter-in-law's health. You must call me Coco,' she said.

I caught Rory's eye and tried not to giggle. Everything was getting out of hand.

Later, when the champagne arrived, Rory said, 'Why have you run out of money? Pa didn't leave you badly off.'

'Of course he didn't, darling, it was just that we had to have central heating for the castle, or we'd have frozen to death.'

'And a sauna bath, and a flagellation room?' said Rory.

'Of course, darling, Buster 'as been used to the best, and he's been shooting four or five times a week and that all adds up. Everything's in such a muddle, we can't decide whether we want to spend the winter in Irasa.' She turned to me. 'I hope you're going to like our island, chérie, those Highland winters can be very terrible, and it's so boring seeing the same old people all the time, and all those sheep. That's what Buster's seeing his friend about.'

'What?' said Rory.

'Buying this aeroplane. He thinks he can get it cheap. Then we can all escape to London, or Paris, or the Riviera when we feel like it.'

Rory raised his eyes to heaven.

'He does need it, darling,' said Coco, almost pleadingly.

'Who told you we were here?'

'Marina did. She telephoned me in Cannes to tell me the news.'

'The bitch,' said Rory.

'Who's Marina?' I asked.

'Marina Maclean,' said Coco. 'At least, she was. Now she's Marina Buchanan. She's just married Hamish Buchanan, who's very rich and more than twice her age. She lives on the island too. I saw her just before we left, Rory. She didn't look very happy. Sort of feverish; she's spending a fortune on clothes and jewellery.'

'That's what comes of trying to marry one's grandfather,' said Rory unemotionally.

'Hamish looks terrible too,' said Coco. 'He's suddenly gone all hip, growing his hair, not eating meat, and dancing in the modern way – trying to keep up with Marina, I suppose. He looks twenty years older. Oh well, it's no use wasting sympathy on Marina. She's made her bed.'

'And now she's about to lie in someone else's,' said Rory.

'Oh, look, here comes Buster.'

'I should like to get dressed,' I said plaintively.

'Oh, nobody dresses for Buster,' said Rory.

Buster Macpherson, when he arrived, turned out to be the kind of man my mother would have gone mad for. He had well-brushed blond hair and blue eyes that let out a perpetual sparkle. He looked like the hero in a boy's comic. He showed a lot of film-star teeth.

He was absolutely not my type. He had none of Rory's explosive feline grace, but he obviously exerted considerable fascination over Coco who, although she didn't look a day over thirty-five, must have been nearing fifty, and a good ten years older than Buster.

'Congratulations, you chaps,' said Buster. He peered through the gloom at me under my sheet.

'May I kiss the bride?' he asked.

'No,' said Rory. 'You'd better watch Buster, he's going through the change of life.'

Buster shot him an unfriendly look, helped himself to a large glass of champagne and sat down.

'Ah, honeymoons, honeymoons,' he said, shaking his head.

'Did you buy that aeroplane?' asked Rory.

'I think so,' said Buster.

Coco gave a crow of delight.

'Where are you going to land it?' asked Rory. 'In the High Street?'

'No,' said Coco. 'We've got a little runway on the island now. I knew I had something to tell you, darling, Finn Maclean is back.'

Rory's eyes narrowed.

'The hell he is. What's he poking his nose into now?'

'He's thrown up his smart Harley Street practice and come back to Irasa as Medical Officer overseeing all the islands,' said Buster. 'He's persuaded the Scottish Medical Board to build him a cottage hospital in the old church hall and buy him an aeroplane so he can hop from island to island.'

'Our own flying doctor,' said Rory. 'Why the hell has he come back?'

'I think he wanted to get out of London,' said Buster. 'His marriage broke up.'

'Not surprised,' said Rory. 'No woman in her right senses could stand him.'

'Finn Maclean is Marina's elder brother,' Coco explained to me. 'Rory and he don't get on, you understand. He never got on with Rory's father either – he kept complaining about the poorness of the tenants.'

'He's an arrogant sod,' said Rory. 'You won't like him.'

'I rather like him,' mused Coco. 'He does not have the bedroom manner, but he is all man.'

Life on Irasa, I decided, certainly wasn't going to be dull. The unpredictable Marina running rings round her ancient husband; Rory feuding with Finn Maclean, who was 'all man'; plus Buster and Coco, a knockabout comedy act in themselves.

'This is a nice hotel,' said Coco meditatively, trying on some of my scent. 'Can you get Buster and me a room here, Rory?'

'No I can't,' said Rory. 'I happen to be on my honeymoon, and I'd like to get on with it without your assistance.'

Chapter Five

After a fortnight, Rory started getting restless and decided to return to England. We stopped in London and booked in at the Ritz. I must say I did enjoy being rich – it was such bliss not having to look at the prices on the menu.

We were in the middle of dinner, I lingering over a crêpe suzette because it was so delicious and Rory halfway through his second bottle of wine, gazing moodily out at Green Park, where the yellow leaves whirled and eddied away from the wet black branches of the plane trees.

Suddenly he summoned a waiter:

'I want my bill,' he said, adding to me, 'finish up that revolting pudding, we're going home tonight.'

'But we're booked in here,' I protested.

'Doesn't matter. If we hurry, we can catch the sleeper.'

'But it's Friday night,' I said, 'we'll never get a bed.'

'Want to bet?' said Rory.

We tore across London in a taxi, fortunately the

streets were deserted, and reached Euston station just five minutes before the train was due to pull out.

'You'll never get on,' said the man at the booking office, 'it's fully booked.'

'What did I tell you,' I grumbled. 'We'll have to sleep in a cattle truck.'

'Stop whining,' said Rory. His eyes roved round the station. Suddenly they lit on one of those motorized trolleys that carry parcels round stations and are always running one over on the platform. It was coming towards us. Stepping forward, Rory flagged it down.

The driver was so surprised he screeched to a halt and watched in amazement as Rory piled our suit-cases on.

'What the bleeding hell do you think you're doing, mate?' he said.

'Drive us up Platform 5 to the first-class sleeper for Glasgow,' said Rory.

'You want me to do what?' asked the driver.

'Go on,' said Rory icily, 'we'll miss the train if you don't hurry.'

He climbed on and pulled me up beside him.

'We can't,' I whispered in horror, 'we'll get arrested.'

'Shut up,' snarled Rory. 'Go on,' he added to the driver, 'we haven't got all bloody day.'

There was something about Rory's manner, a combination of arrogance and an expectation that everyone was going to do exactly what he wanted, that made it almost impossible to oppose him. Grumbling that he'd get the sack for this, the driver set off.

'Can't you go any faster?' asked Rory coldly.

The driver eyed the fiver in Rory's hand.

'You won't get a penny of this,' said Rory, 'unless we catch that train.'

We gathered speed and amazingly stormed through the barrier unopposed and up the platform. Train doors were being slammed as we reached the sleeper.

'Put the luggage on the train,' said Rory to the driver, and strolled over to the attendant who was giving his lists a last-minute check.

I edged away, terrified there was going to be a scene.

'I'm afraid we're booked solid, sir,' I heard the attendant say.

'Didn't the Ritz ring through?' said Rory, his voice taking on that carrying, bitchy, upper-class ring.

'Afraid not, sir,' said the attendant.

'Bloody disgrace. Can't rely on anyone these days. Expect your side slipped up, one of your staff must have forgotten to pass on the message.'

The attendant quailed before Rory's steely gaze. He took off his peak cap and scratched his head.

'Well, what are you going to do about it?' said Rory. 'I'm on my way back from my honeymoon, my wife is quite exhausted. We booked a sleeper and now you're trying to tell me you've given it away.'

As the attendant looked in my direction, I edged further away, trying to merge into a slot machine.

'I really don't know what to say, sir.'

'If you value your job,' said Rory, 'you'd better do something about it.'

Two minutes later an enraged middle-aged couple in pyjamas were being shunted into a carriage down the train.

'I'm awfully sorry, sir,' the attendant was saying.

'You might have thanked him,' I said, sitting down on the bed, and admiring the splendour of our first-class compartment.

'One doesn't thank peasants,' said Rory, pulling off his tie.

Chapter Six

We drove towards the ferry which was to carry us to Irasa. I glanced at Rory hunched over the wheel, demons at his back, the beautiful face sullen with bad temper. His black mood had been coming on for several hours now.

At last we reached the ferry. Under a grey and black sky a mountainous sea came hurtling towards us, thundering, moaning and screaming, and dirty with flying foam.

'Hello, Mr Balniel,' said the man on the gate. 'I wish you'd brought some better weather. It's been raining six weeks in Irasa, even the seagulls are wearing sou'westers.'

On the boat the sky darkened noticeably, the temperature dropped and the gulls were blown sideways like pieces of rag in the wind.

I'm not sure Scotland's quite me, I later thought disloyally, as we bumped along one-track roads with occasional glimpses of sulky-looking sea.

On our left a huge forbidding castle lowered out of the mist.

'Nice little weekend cottage,' I said.

'That's where Buster and Coco live,' said Rory. 'This is us.'

I suppose it had once been a rather large lodge to the castle – a grey stone two-storey house, hung with creeper, surrounded by a wild, forsaken garden.

I started to quote Swinburne, but Rory shot me such a look.

I shut up.

I decided not to make any flash remarks, either, about being carried over the threshold. Rory was extraordinarily tense, as though he was expecting something horrible.

He certainly got it. I've never seen such shambles inside a house; broken bottles, knocked-down lamps and tables, glasses strewn all over the floor, dust everywhere, thick cobwebs. The bedrooms looked as though someone had used them as ash-trays, the fridge like a primeval forest, and someone had written 'Goodbye forever' in lipstick on the mirror.

The house consisted of a huge studio, a drawing-room almost entirely lined with books, two bedrooms upstairs, a kitchen and a bathroom; all were in absolute chaos.

'Oh God,' said Rory. 'I left a message with my mother to get someone to clean the place up.'

'It's all right,' I said faintly, 'it'll only take a few hundred years to put to rights.'

'I'm not having you whisking around like Snow White,' snapped Rory. 'We'll sleep at the castle tonight. I'll get someone to come in tomorrow.'

I looked out of the bedroom window. The view was sensational. The house grew out of a two hundred and fifty foot cliff which dropped straight down to the sea.

'I hope we don't fall out too often,' I joked weakly, then I saw a cellophane packet of flowers on the bed. 'Oh look,' I said, 'someone remembered us.' Then I shivered with horror as I realized it was a funeral wreath of lilies. Inside the envelope, on a black-edged card, was written 'Welcome home, darlings'. 'How beastly,' I said in a trembling voice. 'Who could have done that?'

Rory picked up the card. 'Some joker who's got it in for me.'

'But that's horrible.'

'And quite unimportant,' he said, tearing up the card. He opened the window and threw the wreath out, so it spun round and round and crashed on the rocks below.

Startled I looked into his face, which glowed suddenly with some malice I couldn't place.

'Come here,' he said softly.

He pulled me against him, pushing my head down on his shoulder, one hand tracing my arm, the other moving over my body. Then he smiled and closed his long fingers round my wrist where the pulse pounded.

'Poor little baby,' he whispered. He could always do this to me. 'Let's go next door,' and he pulled me into the dusty spare room with the huge window on to the road and began to kiss me.

'Shouldn't we draw the curtains?' I muttered. 'They can see us from the road.'

'So what?' he murmured.

Suddenly I heard a scrunch of wheels on the road outside. Swinging round I saw a blue Porsche flash by. In the driving seat was a red-headed girl who gazed in at us, a mixture of despair and hatred in her huge, haunted eyes.

I enjoyed staying at the castle, living in baronial comfort, and making the acquaintance of Rory's black labrador Walter Scott, who had been living with Buster's gamekeeper while he had been away. He was a charming dog, sleek, amiable, incurably greedy and not as well trained as Rory would have liked.

After a few days we went back to live in Rory's house (very pretty it looked, after it had been cleaned up) and began marriage proper.

I didn't find it easy. I was determined to be one of those wonderful little homemakers putting feminine touches everywhere but, as Rory remarked, the only feminine touches I added were dripping pants and stockings, and mascara on his towel.

I tried to cook, too. I once cooked moussaka, and we didn't eat until one o'clock in the morning. But

Rory, who was used to Coco's French expertise, was not impressed.

I also took hours over the washing. There weren't any launderettes in Irasa, and then it lay around for days in pillowcases waiting to be ironed; and Rory never seemed to have clean underpants when he needed them.

After a couple of weeks he said, quite gently, 'With all the cobwebs, we seem to have formed a spider sanctuary here. You're obviously not into housework, so I've hired a char, four days a week, and she can iron my shirts too.'

I felt humiliated but enormously relieved.

The char, Mrs Mackie, turned out to be a mixed blessing. She was wonderful at cleaning, but a terrible gossip, and obviously irritated Rory out of his mind. As soon as she arrived he used to disappear into the mountains to paint, and she and I sat round drinking cider and talking.

'I've got a wicked bad leg,' she said one morning. 'I shall have to go and see Dr Maclean.'

'Finn Maclean?' I said.

She nodded.

'What's his sister Marina like?'

'She's no right in the head, although I shouldn't say it. The old Macleans never had any money. Dr Maclean, her father, was a gud doctor, but he dinna know about saving. Marina married this old man for his riches, and it's dancing him into his grave she is. Perhaps now young Dr Maclean's come back he'll keep her in order.'

'Why's he come back when he was doing so well in London?'

She shrugged. 'Irasa has an enchantment. They all come back in the end.'

Chapter Seven

Irasa – Island of the Blessed, or of the Cursed. I could understand why none of them could escape its spell, and why only here could Rory find the real inspiration for his painting.

The countryside took your breath away; it was as though the autumn was pulling out all the stops before succumbing to the harshness of the Highland winter. Bracken singed the entire hillsides the colour of a red setter, the turning horse chestnuts blazed yellow, the acacias pale acid green.

With Rory painting all day, Walter Scott and I had plenty of time to wander about and explore. The island was fringed with wooded points like a starfish. Out of the ten or so big houses, on one point lived Rory and me, on another Buster and Coco, on another Finn Maclean and on yet another Marina and Hamish. The islanders' white cottages were dotted between.

One afternoon in late October, I walked down to Penlorren, the island's tiny capital.

Penlorren was a strange sleepy little town,

exquisitely pretty, like a northern St Tropez. Wooded hills ringed the bay, but the main street was an arc of coloured houses, dark green, pink, white and duck-egg blue. In the boats the fishermen were sorting their slippery silver catch into boxes.

As I walked about I was aware of being watched. Suddenly I looked round and there was the blue Porsche parked by the side of the road: the same red-headed girl was watching me with great undefended eyes. I smiled at her, but she started up the car and stormed down the main street, scattering villagers.

'Who's that?' I asked a nearby fisherman, and somehow knew he was going to answer, 'Marina Maclean.'

I'd forgotten to get any potatoes and I went back to the main store. Three old biddies were having a yap, they didn't hear me come in.

'Did you see Rory Balniel's wee bride?' said one.

'Pur lassie, so bonny,' said the second. 'She might as well have married the divil.'

'There'll be trouble ahead,' said the third. 'Now young Dr Maclean's back again.'

Then they suddenly saw me, coughed, and started taking a great deal of interest in a sack of turnips.

Chapter Eight

The feeling of unease I'd had since the first night of my honeymoon grew stronger. Another fortnight passed. I had to stop fooling myself that our marriage was going well.

I was so besotted with Rory I wanted to touch him all the time; not just bed touching, but holding hands and lying tucked into his back at night like two spoons in a silver box. But Rory seemed to have no desire to come near me, except when he made love to me, which was getting less and less often.

I tried to kid myself he was worrying about work. I knew about geniuses, secretive, more temperamental, of finer grain than ordinary mortals, and more easily upset. I tried to talk to him about painting, but he said I didn't understand what he was doing and, anyway, talking about it ruined it.

I was in the kitchen one morning. I had learned to be quiet when work was going badly, the clatter of a pan could drive him mad. He wandered in yawning, rubbing a hand through his hair, looking so handsome with his sleepy, sulky face, I felt my stomach tighten.

'Do you want some coffee?'

'Yes, please.'

Feeling more like a normal wife, I went into the kitchen, started percolating coffee, and sighed inwardly for the days when Nina and I had lived on Nescafé. I thought of the beautiful, haunted girl in the blue Porsche.

'I keep seeing Marina Buchanan,' I said.

Rory looked at me. 'So?'

'Not to speak to,' I stammered. 'She's terribly beautiful. Shall we ask them to dinner?'

'I'm sure they'd enjoy your cooking.'

I bit my lip. I didn't want a row.

'I'm sorry about my cooking. I am trying.'

'Sure you are, extremely trying.'

'Rory, please, what's the matter? What have I done? You haven't laid a finger on me for at least four days.'

'You can count up to five? That is encouraging,' said Rory acidly.

'Most newly weds are at it all the time,' I said.

'We might be, if you were less unimaginative in bed. I'm surprised all your exes didn't expect something a bit more exciting.'

I jumped back as though he'd hit me. Sometimes there was a destructive force about Rory.

'God, you bastard,' I whispered. 'If you were a bit more encouraging, I might be less unimaginative.

And if I'm no good in bed, why the hell didn't you say so in the beginning?'

'I was probably too drunk to notice,' he said.

'I hate you!' I screamed.

I stormed out of the room, rushed upstairs and threw myself on the bed, bursting into tears. Five minutes later I heard a door slam and his car driving off down the road.

I cried for hours. 'He's only doing it to hurt me,' I kept saying, trying to reassure myself. I got up, washed my face and wondered what to do next.

I thumbed through a magazine. You could have pulled corks with the models' hair. I liked music but you couldn't listen to records all day. I supposed I could put on a deeply felt hat and go for a walk.

I sat up, dismayed: I realized I was bored. No-one was more aware than I that boredom was a mark of inadequacy. People with inner resources didn't get bored. No; as Rory had discovered, I'd got hidden shallows. I went to the fridge and ate half a tin of potato salad.

There was a knock on the door. Delighted, I leapt to my feet and rushed to open it. There stood Marina Buchanan, quivering with nerves as if even now she might turn and run. She was lovely, if haunted, in a red coat and long black boots, her shining Titian hair blowing in the wind like a shampoo commercial. Her mouth was large and drooping, her face deathly pale, and there were huge blue shadows underneath her extraordinary eyes. I understood everything my mother had told me about Garbo. I wished I hadn't eaten that potato salad.

'Hello,' she said. 'I'm Marina Buchanan.'

'I know,' I said, 'I'm Emily Balniel.'

'I know,' she said, 'Coco sent me a postcard suggesting we should get together.'

'Oh, how lovely,' I said. 'Come in and have some coffee or something.'

'How nice it looks,' she said, gazing in admiration at the drawing-room.

'Let's have a drink, not coffee,' I said. 'I know one shouldn't at this hour of the morning, but it's such a celebration having someone to talk to.'

We had the most tremendous gossip. She didn't seem haunted any more, just slightly malicious and very funny. She adored Coco, she said, but couldn't stand Buster. She wasn't very complimentary about her husband either.

'He's terrific between the balance sheets, so it means I can have everything I want, but I'm getting a bit fed up playing Tinker, Tailor with the caviar . . .'

I giggled.

'Where's Rory?' she said.

'Out painting.'

She looked at me closely. 'You look tired. Has Rory been giving you a hard time?'

'Of course not,' I said firmly.

'Don't get sore, I'm not being critical, just realistic.

Rory's divine-looking, he exudes sex-appeal the way other men breathe out carbon dioxide, and he's got terrific qualities.' She paused as if trying to think what they were. 'But he can be difficult. Where other people make scenes, Rory makes three-act plays. When he's upset he takes it out on other people, he always has. My brother, Finn, is difficult, but in a more predictable way, and he's not spoilt like Rory, or bitchy either. Rory's always trying to send Finn up, but it doesn't work because Finn couldn't care less. And although Rory's always had everything, somehow Finn makes him feel inadequate. They hate each other's guts, you know,' she added in satisfaction. 'There's bound to be fireworks – the island isn't big enough for both of them.'

She got up and wandered round the room. I looked at that wild, unstable loveliness, and wondered what had possessed her to marry an old man when she could have had anyone.

'Why don't you both come to dinner on Thursday?' I said.

'That'd be lovely, but you'd better ask Rory first.'

At that moment Rory walked in.

'Hello, Rory,' she said softly, and then when he didn't answer immediately, she went rattling on.

'It would be nice if you could learn to say hello sometimes, Rory. With six months' practice you might even learn to say, "It's a lovely day".'

I steeled myself, wondering what sort of mood he

was in now, but he turned round, then came over and kissed me on the mouth, quite hard.

'Hello, baby, have you missed me?'

'Oh yes,' I said, snuggling against him, feeling weak with relief.

Then he looked across at Marina, and ice crept into his voice. 'Hello, Mrs Buchanan, how's marriage? Still making Hamish while the sun shines?'

I giggled. 'We've been having a lovely gossip. I've asked Marina and Hamish to dinner here on Thursday.'

Chapter Nine

I was determined the dinner party would be a success. For the next three days I cooked, polished and panicked, determined Rory should be proud of me. On the afternoon of the day they were coming, I was well ahead; the house gleamed like a telly ad., all the food was done. The only thing we needed was lots of flowers. There were none in the garden, but I'd noticed some gorgeous roses in a garden down the road. I set off, still in my nightie – flimsy and black. I'd been so busy I hadn't even bothered to get dressed.

It was a warm day for the time of year, the wet grass felt delicious beneath my bare feet. I ran past ancient fruit trees and overgrown shrubberies, and started to pick great armfuls of roses.

I was just bending over, tearing off one huge red rose with my teeth, when I heard a furious voice behind me.

'What the hell do you think you're doing?'

I jumped out of my skin and spun round, aghast, the rose in my teeth like Carmen. A man towered over me. He must have been in his early thirties, he had dark red hair curling over his collar, a battered, freckled, high-complexioned face, a square jaw, a broken nose, and angry hazel eyes. His face was seamed with tiredness, his mouth set in an ugly line – but it was still a powerful, compelling, unforgettable face.

'Don't you realize this is private property?'

Then I twigged. This must be Finn Maclean. I stared at him, fascinated. It was not often one came face to face with a legend.

'Didn't you know you were trespassing?'

'Yes, I did. I'm terribly sorry, but no-one's ever picked any flowers here before. It seems such a waste to leave them. I didn't know you'd turn up.'

'Evidently,' he said, taking in my extreme state of undress. 'Who are you, anyway?' he asked.

'Emily,' I muttered. 'Emily Balniel.'

For a second there was a flicker of emotion other than anger in his face. Was it pity or contempt?

'I'd have thought Rory was rich enough to afford his own roses. I suppose you've picked up all his habits of doing and taking exactly what you like?'

'No, I haven't, and you can keep your rotten roses,' I said, and threw the whole lot at his feet.

Chapter Ten

Although I was seething with rage, I didn't mention the incident to Rory when I got back; he was in too bad a temper. I started tidying the drawing-room.

'I wish you wouldn't hum nervously when you do things,' he said. 'Stop fiddling with those leaves, too, they look awful enough as it is.'

'You only notice them because Marina's coming.'

I went into the kitchen and slammed the door. First Finn, now Rory. I thought I was going to cry, but it would only make my eyes red, so I took a large swig of cooking wine instead. Then I suddenly realized I hadn't put out any napkins, and had to rush upstairs, pull them out of the laundry basket and iron them on the carpet.

Maddeningly, Marina and Hamish arrived twenty minutes early, so I had no time to tart myself up. I wondered if Marina did it deliberately. She looked staggering in a slinky, backless blue dress which matched her eyes. But even I was unprepared for Hamish. He must have been close on sixty, with nudging eyes, an avid grin and yellow teeth. But he'd got himself up like an out-of-date raver: thinning grey locks clustering over his forehead and down his back, sideboards laddering his wrinkled cheeks, a white chamois leather smock, lots of beads and jeans several sizes too small for him. He looked like an awful old goat. Rory, who looked devastating in a grey satin shirt, couldn't stop laughing.

'Marina, darling, what have you done to him?' he said in an undertone. 'He looks like an octogenarian ton-up boy.'

'I've made an old man very hippy,' said Marina, and giggled.

'Don't you like his smock? A touch of white is so flattering close to the face when you reach a certain age.'

They were convulsed with mirth. I think I would have been shocked by their malice if Hamish hadn't been so awful, lecherous and pleased with himself.

We all drank a great deal before dinner.

'I'm thinking of growing a beard,' Hamish said.

'I don't like beards on boys or girls,' said Marina.

'Are you still taking singing lessons?' Rory asked Marina.

'I drive over to Edinburgh once a fortnight. It's a long way, but worth it. I usually stay the night. It gives Hamish a break.'

'To get up to mischief,' said Hamish, giving me a wink that nearly dislocated his eyelid.

No one really noticed the dinner, not even when one of my false eyelashes fell in the soup. Marina ate nothing; Hamish was obviously frightened his trousers were going to split. Rory never ate much, anyway. I cleared the plates and served each course; I might have been a waitress. Walter Scott was having a field day finishing up in the kitchen.

There were strange undercurrents. I felt as though I was watching a suspense story on television where I'd missed the beginning and couldn't quite work out what was going on. Hamish rubbed his skinny leg against mine. Any moment he'd get a fork stuck into it.

After dinner Marina turned on the gramophone. She and Hamish danced. Hamish looked absurd, flailing about like a scarecrow in a gale. Marina moved like a maenad, her red hair flying, her face transformed by the soft light.

Rory sat watching her, his face expressionless. He had been drinking heavily all evening.

Finally she flopped down beside him on the sofa.

'Did you ever finish that water-colour of the harbour?'

He nodded. 'It's in the studio.'

'May I come and see it?'

They went next door.

Hamish looked dreadful now, grey and exhausted. He went off to the loo and I wandered into the studio to see the painting they were talking about.

Suddenly, I froze with horror. They hadn't bothered to turn on the studio light, and were standing near the window in the moonlight.

Marina stood there vibrating, a foot away from Rory; her face glowed like a pale flame.

'Why did you marry her?' Her voice dropped an octave.

'Oh come on,' Rory said, 'let's say I wasn't wanted any more.'

'To punish me, to put me on the rack. You can't believe I married Hamish for anything but his money, but she's something entirely different.'

She turned on her heel and was coming towards me; it was as though I was frozen in some terrible nightmare.

'Marina, wait,' I heard Rory say.

'Oh go to hell,' she said, but the longing and ache in her voice were quite unmistakable.

She didn't see me as she came into the drawing-room. 'Hamish, I want to go home,' she snapped.

Her face was turned away from him, only I could see it was wet with tears. Rory didn't even bother to come out and say goodbye to them. I went back into the studio, my legs hardly holding me up.

'Rory,' I said, 'I think we ought to have things out.'

'I've nothing to have out, nothing.'

I realized he'd reached that pitch of drunkenness that was about to explode into violence, but I didn't care.

'What's going on between you and Marina? Why was she hanging around when we arrived? It was she who sent the wreath, wasn't it? And her whom you rang up the first night of our honeymoon? I want to know what it's all about.'

'Nothing, nothing. We were brought up together, that's all. Anyway,' he snarled, 'you asked her to dinner. Now get out of my way.' He pushed me aside. 'I'm going to sleep in the spare room, and don't come crawling into my bed in the middle of the night.'

Chapter Eleven

I didn't sleep at all. I lay trembling with panic,
clutching Walter Scott's solid body, my mind reeling
from possibility to possibility. At dawn I tried to
be rational. Rory and Marina had probably been
childhood sweethearts, and he'd been piqued
when she married Hamish. After all, it was me he'd
married.

Next morning I came down, washed up, and tried
to be brave about my hangover.

What would please Rory most? I decided to clean
out his studio.

He came down at midday. He looked terrible. He
must have been hungover down to his toes, but,
glass in hand, he was making a nice recovery. I was
standing on a ladder dusting a shelf.

'Hello, darling,' I said, brightly.

'What are you doing?'

'Dusting.'

'Why the hell can't Miss Mackie do that? You'll
only muddle everything up, for Christ's sake.'

'Please don't let's quarrel. I'm sorry for the things

I said. I didn't mean them. I couldn't bear another night like last night.'

'You can always leave,' he said brutally.

'I don't want to leave. I love you.'

His face softened. 'Do you now? Well come down off that stupid ladder then,' and, catching my ankles, he ran his hands slowly up my legs.

'I'll just dust this last folder,' I said, steadying myself on the shelf.

'Put that down,' said Rory, his voice suddenly icy.

Startled, I swayed on my high ladder.

'I said put it down.'

Purely out of nerves, I let the folder slip from my hands and crash to the floor. Hastily I scrambled down and knelt to pick it up.

Rory reached it at the same time as me, his hand on my arm like a vice.

'Ow!' I yelped.

'Leave it,' he snarled, but it was too late.

Spilling out of the folder were the most beautiful drawings. The naked model smiling that secret, comehither smile was unmistakably Marina.

We looked at the paintings scattered round our feet. Marina in her lush beauty mocked me a hundred times over.

'Well?' I said.

'It's your fault. I told you not to touch that file.'

'They're very good, very life-like indeed,' I said slowly, trying to keep my voice from trembling. 'I'm sure you didn't paint these from imagination.'

'Of course I didn't. I wanted to do some nudes last summer, and there are only a limited number of people on the island who'll take their clothes off. You can hardly see Buster or Hamish stripping down to the buff and sitting around for hours on end. Anyway, as I've said before, it's damn all to do with you what I did before I was married.'

'Or what you do after you're married,' I said bitterly.

Rory drained his drink and poured himself another one.

'Rory,' I said slowly, 'this is important. Do you love me at all?'

Rory looked bored. 'Depends how you define love.'

How could I explain that he was the most beautiful man I'd ever seen, that my tongue suddenly got stuck in my throat when I saw the set of his shoulders, that I spent all day wanting him.

'Oh Rory,' I said, appalled. 'Can't you try and be a bit more loving?'

'Why?' he said, logically.

'Why did you marry me then?'

He looked at me reflectively, 'I'm beginning to wonder.'

I gave a gasp. God, he could be vicious.

'What shall we do about it, then?' I said.

'Do?' he exploded. 'Do let me work, that's enough for me.'

'But not enough for me!' I screamed, and brushed blindly past him.

'Where are you going?' he said.

'Out.'

'Well, for God's sake come back in a less destructive mood.'

And so our marriage began to deteriorate. It wasn't helped by the rain which started to fall the next day, and continued for weeks. Rory passed the time in painting, I in sulking, then in trying to win Rory round, then in sulking again.

I suppose I was pretty disagreeable myself, I complained steadily about the weather and how bored I was. At first I made an attempt to stop myself, then I didn't try to stop myself, then I found I couldn't. Emily – the fishwife.

That crack about being lousy in bed had gone home too. I wrote off to London for a sexy black cut-out nightie, and a book on how to undress in front of your husband. It showed you how to swing your bra round like a football rattle, and slide your pants off in one go.

I tried it on Rory one evening, but he merely raised his eyebrows and asked me if I'd been at the gin. As the weeks passed, he didn't lay a finger on me. I was desperately unhappy and cried a great deal when he wasn't around. I kept telling myself that when he'd assembled enough canvases for the exhibition we'd be like a couple of love birds, but I didn't really believe it.

I spent most of my time corrupting Walter Scott. Rory was a great believer that dogs should be treated like dogs and kept outside. I kept bringing him in and feeding him in between meals and cuddling him – I needed a few allies.

Gradually Walter invaded the house. He started off sleeping in the kitchen, then moved to the foot of the stairs, then to the landing outside our bedroom. At dawn he would steal in and try to climb on our bed. Invariably Rory, who was a light sleeper, would wake up and throw him out.

'Walter Scott suffers from being an only dog,' he was fond of saying.

'Blood is thicker than Walter,' I said.

'Nothing is thicker than Walter,' said Rory.

Chapter Twelve

In November, later than expected, Coco and Buster came back.

Buster brought his new private plane, which he landed perilously on the sward outside the castle, terrifying the life out of the islanders and the local sheep, and nearly depositing himself, three labradors, gun cases, rod boxes and several hundred tons of pigskin luggage, in the sea.

'Pity,' said Rory. 'Never mind, there'll be plenty of other opportunities. In the old days he used to come up by train from Euston and take the dogs to lamp-posts as the train waited interminably at Crewe.'

Coco arrived in rip-roaring form and swept Rory and me into a round of gaiety, meeting people on the island and the mainland. It was a frightful strain trying to keep up the appearance that I was blissfully happy.

A few days later, Marina and Hamish asked us back to dinner. I was amazed and irritated to discover she was a very good cook, and had decorated

Hamish's huge, stark house with a wild elegance I could never achieve in a million years of poring over *House and Garden.*

The drawing-room had grey silk walls and flame-red curtains, and I felt sure, had been chosen to compliment Marina's colouring.

'Oh it's lovely,' I said wistfully, 'you ought to go into interior decorating.'

'Emily's an inferior decorator,' said Rory.

In my attempt to make our bedroom more feminine, I'd started painting it but had got bored in the middle. The colour, too, was disastrous. It looked all right on the chart but once on the wall turned out an appalling E–K directory pink.

I felt very overdressed that evening, too. Trying to compete with Marina, I'd put on a see-through blouse and a long skirt. Marina of course was wearing jeans.

There was another couple to dinner – Deidre and Calen Macdonald. She was a commanding, big-boned woman with a ringing voice. He had a handsome, dissipated face, roving grey eyes, and had obviously married her for her money. He turned out to be a shooting friend of Buster's and made an absolute dead set at me.

'I can't claim to be a gentleman, but I've always preferred blondes,' he said cornering me on the sofa as soon as we were introduced, 'and you really are gorgeous.'

The intensity with which he gazed at my see-through blouse threw me off balance – I folded my arms firmly to cover up what I could.

'Er – do you do anything for a living?' I said, casting around for something to say.

'Good God, no. I realized very early on that I was quite incapable of supporting myself, so I married old Deidre instead; she's a pretty full time job, but I do get the odd afternoon off while she's sitting on committees. How about you?'

'I've only been married seven weeks,' I said firmly.

'So disillusion hasn't set in yet. Pretty tricky customer Rory, I admire you if you can handle him. He runs rings round poor Buster. Is he still drinking too much?'

'Hardly at all,' I said, out of the corner of my eye watching Rory go to Marina's sidetable, and help himself to a second very large glass of whisky.

'Very loyal and proper,' said Calen. 'I must say you really are extremely attractive, I wish you'd stop sitting with your arms folded like a rugger player so I could appreciate you properly. Promise me that if you ever decide to be unfaithful to Rory, I can have first refusal.'

I tried to look disapproving, but after Rory's indifference of the past few weeks, it was such heaven to be chatted up. I was sure Marina had invited Calen on purpose. But although he flirted outrageously with me all evening, I felt terribly depressed that Rory wasn't betraying a spark of jealousy.

'So nice for you to find someone of your own

mental age to play with, Emily,' was all he said afterwards.

As the weeks passed, we often encountered Marina and Hamish at parties. Marina and Rory so studiously avoided each other that I wondered if they were meeting on the sly.

Occasionally I saw her loathsome brother, Finn Maclean, driving round the island, obviously far too preoccupied with building his beastly hospital to waste time on parties.

In December, Coco slipped down some steps at the castle after a boozy evening and sprained her ankle. Next day she rang up, saying she was bored, would I come over and see her. On my way I drove into Penlorren to find her some nice escapist novel from the bookshop.

Having parked my car in the main street, I started browsing through some romances. Oh dear, the lovely things that happened to those heroines. Why didn't Rory feel like that about me?

Finally, I heard a cough behind me. The owner wanting to shut up shop.

Hastily I bought the book and wandered dreamily into the main street, through the mist and rain. A man was standing by my car. There was something heroic about the way he stood, the massive breadth of the shoulders, the hair curling over the collar of his battered sheepskin coat like Michelangelo's David.

Instinctively, I unhitched the long lock of hair from behind my ear and let it fall seductively over my eyes. Then I realized the man was Finn Maclean, and he was blazingly angry.

'Is this your car?'

'Yes . . . at least, it's Rory's.'

'Can't you read?'

He seized my arm and swung me round to face a notice on a garage door. It said, *Doctor's car, please leave free.*

'Oh,' I said. 'Well, in London, people often put notices like that on their garage doors even if they're not doctors, just to keep people away.'

'This is not London,' he snapped, and in terms of the most blistering invective, proceeded to tell me exactly what he thought of Londoners who came to live in the country, and me in particular, and didn't I realize that people could be dying because people like me parked their cars in places like this. Finally I got fed up.

'It strikes me,' I said, 'that while you've been rabbiting on and on and on about my criminal responsibility, at least twenty more people could have died. Admittedly, a few of them may have been Chinese. In fact, if all the people who died while people like you were blowing their cool all over the islands were laid end to end . . .'

'Don't be fatuous,' snapped Finn. 'There's obviously no point in trying to get anything through to you. You'd better move your car.'

Of course, the beastly thing wouldn't start. Eventually I remembered to let out the clutch, and it shot forward in a series of agonizing jerks.

'Louse, swine, monster,' I muttered to myself, as I drove to the castle. No wonder Rory and he couldn't stand each other.

Chapter Thirteen

I found Coco lying in bed looking beautiful as always, but very tired. Someone had brought her some lilies, and she'd buried her face in them. Her nose was bright yellow with pollen. She was obviously in considerable pain, but greeted me with her usual zest.

'Help yourself to a drink, chérie, and get me one. Buster has gone shooting. Every day now he shoot, pop, pop, bang, bang. I find it very boring. I 'ave live in Scotland nearly thirty years, and still I do not find the plus-four sexy. Admittedly, Buster 'ave very good legs. A seagull excruciated on his coat just as he was leaving. He was very angry.'

I giggled. Coco could always cheer me up. We gossiped for half an hour, then I reverted to the subject I could never ignore for long, even though it crucified me to talk about it.

'Have you seen Marina?' I asked.

Coco raised her eyes to heaven.

'Yes I 'ave. That's a marriage going on the rocks. We had dinner with them the other night, she and

Hamish. I gave her a lecture. I said "You are not making Hamish happy like Emily is making my Rory happy."' (I winced at that bit.) 'And Marina laugh in my face. Sometimes I think she is a bit touchy in her head. She is so different from her brother, Finn. He's so kind and down-to-earth, and such a wonderful doctor.'

That moment a maid banged on the door.

'Dr Maclean's here, madam,' she said.

'Show him in,' said Coco, excitedly.

'Oh God, he was as mad as a boiled squirrel last time I saw him,' I said.

But Coco wasn't listening, she was too busy combing her hair and spraying on scent.

In marched Finn Maclean.

'Talk of the devil,' said Coco in delight. 'I was just singing your praises to Emily, telling her what a wonderful doctor you were – so kind and understanding. I shouldn't think anything rattles you, does it, Finn?'

'No,' I said acidly, 'I should think it's always Dr Maclean who does the rattling.'

Finn turned round and saw me. His face hardened slightly. 'Oh it's you,' he said.

'I didn't know you knew Emily,' said Coco. 'Isn't she pretty? And so good for Rory.'

'I'm sure they're ideally matched,' said Finn.

The sarcasm was entirely lost on Coco, who beamed at us both.

'Let's have a look at your ankle,' Finn said.

Coco stretched out one of her beautiful, smooth, brown legs. The ankle was very black and swollen. Although Finn handled it with amazing delicacy, she drew her breath in.

'Sore is it?' he said gently.

She nodded, catching her lip.

'Poor old thing. Never mind, you've still got one perfect ankle,' he said, getting up. 'No reason why the other shouldn't be as right as rain in a few weeks.'

'What's right about rain?' I said gloomily, looking out of the window.

'Still, I'd like to X-ray it,' Finn went on, ignoring me. 'I'll send an ambulance to pick you up later. It'll jolt you less than a car.'

'I must go,' I said. 'I've got to cook Rory's supper.'

'Finn will give you a lift,' said Coco.

'I've got a car,' I said quickly.

It was very cold outside and I shivered: I didn't want to leave the cosy warmth of the castle for one of Rory's black moods. Finn Maclean got something out of the pocket of his overcoat.

'I should have thought it was a bit early on in your marriage to escape into tripe like this,' he said, handing it to me. It was the romantic novel I'd intended to give Coco.

Chapter Fourteen

Coco's ankle was X-rayed, bound up and she was ordered to rest it. Just before Christmas, however, Maisie Downleesh (one of Coco's friends) decided to give a ball to celebrate her daughter Diney's engagement. We were all invited.

There is something about the idea of a ball that lifts the spirits, however low one is. I suppose it's the excitement; buying a new dress, new make-up, a new hairstyle and settling down in front of the mirror in an attempt to magic oneself into the most glamorous girl in the room. In the past, a ball had offered all the excitement of the unknown, opportunity knocking. This time, I hoped, it would be a chance to make myself beautiful enough to win back Rory.

The ball was being held at the Downleeshes' castle on the mainland. Coco, Buster, Rory and I were all to stay there. In the morning I took the car across the ferry and drove to Edinburgh to buy a new dress. In the afternoon I had to pick up a couple who were coming to the dance from London, then drive back and pick up Rory from the Irasa Ferry, and then drive on to the Downleeshes'.

I was determined that a new me was going to emerge, so gorgeous that every Laird would be mad with desire for me. I spent a frenzied morning rushing from shop to shop. Eventually in a back street I tracked down a gloriously tarty, pale pink dress, skin tight over the bottom, slashed at the front and plunging back and front.

It had been reduced in a sale because there was a slight mark on the navel, and because, the assistant said with a sniff, there was no call for that sort of garment in Edinburgh.

I tried it on; it was wildly sexy.

'A little tight over the barkside, don't ye thenk,' said the assistant, who was keen to steer me into black velvet at three times the price.

'That's just how I like it,' I said.

It was a bit long too, so I went and bought new six-inch high shoes, and then went to the hair-dressers and had a pink rinse put on my hair. I never do things by three-quarters. All in all it was a bit of a rush getting to the airport.

The Frayns were waiting when I arrived – I recognized them a mile off. He was one of those braying chinless telegraph poles in a dung-coloured tweed jacket. She was a typical ex-deb, with flat ears from permanently wearing a headscarf, and a very long right arm from lugging suitcases to Paddington every weekend to go home to Mummy. She had blue eyes, mouse hair and one of those pink and white complexions that nothing, not rough winds nor drinking and dancing till dawn, can destroy. They were also nauseatingly besotted with one another. Every sentence began 'Charles thinks' or 'Fiona thinks'. And they kept roaring with laughter at each other's jokes, like hyenas. She also had that terrible complacency that often overtakes newly married women and stems from relief at having hooked a man, and being uncritically adored by him.

She was quite nice about me being late, but there was a lot of talk about stopping at a telephone box on the dot of 6.30 to ring up Nanny and find out how little Caroline was getting on; and did I think we'd get there in time to change?

'It's the first time I've been separated from Caroline,' she said. 'I do hope Nanny can cope.'

She sat in the front beside me, he sat in the back; they held hands all the time. Why didn't they both get in the back and neck?

It was a bitterly cold day. Stripped, black trees were etched on the skyline. The heavy brown sky was full of snow. Shaggy forelocked heads of the cows tossed in the gloom as they cropped the sparse turf. Just before we reached the ferry to pick up Rory and Walter Scott, it started snowing in earnest. I had hoped Rory and I could have a truce for the evening – but I was an hour late which didn't improve his temper.

Fiona, who had evidently known Rory as a child,

went into a flurry of what's happened to old so and so, and who did so and so marry.

Rory answered her in monosyllables; he had snow melting in his hair and paint on his hands.

'Too awful,' she went on. 'Did you know Annie Richmond's father threw himself under a taxi in the rush hour in Knightsbridge?'

'Lucky to find one at that hour,' said Rory, looking broodingly at the snowflakes swarming like great bees on the windscreen.

I giggled. Rory looked at me, and then noticed my hair.

'Jesus,' he said under his breath.

'Do you like it?' I said nervously.

'No,' he said and turned up the wireless full blast to drown Fiona's chatter.

Suddenly she gave a scream.

'Oh look, there's a telephone box. Could you stop a minute, Rory, so I can telephone Nanny.'

Rory raised his eyes to heaven.

She got out of the car and, giving little shrieks, ran through the snow. Through the glass of the telephone box I could see her smiling fatuously, forcing 10p pieces into the telephone box. Rory didn't reply to Charles' desultory questions about shooting. His nails were so bitten that his drumming fingers made little sound on the dashboard.

A quarter of an hour later, Fiona returned.

'Well?' said Charles.

'She's fine, but she's missing us,' she said. 'She

brought up most of her lunch but she's just had two rusks and finished all her bottle, so Nanny thinks she's recovered.'

Rory scurled off through the snow, his hands clenched on the wheel.

'What b-awful weather,' said Fiona, looking out of the window. 'You really must start a family very soon, Emily,' she went on. 'It gives a completely new dimension to one's life. I think one's awfully selfish really until one has children.'

'Parents,' said Rory, 'should always be seen and not heard.'

Punctuated by giggles and murmurs of 'Oh Charles' from the back, we finally reached the turrets and gables and great blackened keep of Downleesh Castle. The windows threw shafts of light on to the snow which was gathering thickly on the surrounding fir trees and yews. The usual cavalcade of terriers and labradors came pounding out of the house to welcome us. Walter Scott was dragged off protesting by a footman to be given his dinner in the kitchen.

In the dark panelled hall, great banks of holly were piled round the suits of armour, the spears and the banners. We had a drink before going upstairs. Diney, Lady Downleesh's daughter, who'd just got engaged, fell on Fiona's neck and they both started yapping about weddings and babies.

We were taken to our bedroom down long, draughty passages to the West Tower. In spite of a fire in the grate, it was bitterly cold.

I found when I got there that my suitcase had been unpacked and all my clothes laid out neatly on the mildewed fourposter, including an old bone of Walter Scott's and a half-eaten bar of chocolate I had stuffed into my suitcase at the last moment. On the walls were pictures of gun-dogs coming out of the bracken, their mouths full of feathers.

I missed Walter. Sometimes in those awful long silences I had with Rory I found it a relief to jabber away to him.

'Can he come upstairs?' I said.

'No,' said Rory.

In the bookshelves was a book called *A Modern Guide to Pig Husbandry.* 'Perhaps I should read it,' I said, 'it might give me some advice about being married to a pig,'

Across the passage were the unspeakable Frayns. They had already hogged the bathroom, and judging from the sound of splashing and giggling, it wasn't just a bath they were having. I realized I was jealous of their happiness and involvement. I wanted Rory to start every sentence 'Emily says' and roar with laughter at my jokes.

I took ages over dressing, painting my face as carefully as Rory painted any of his pictures. My pink dress looked pretty sensational; I put a ruby brooch Coco had given me over the mark on the navel. It was certainly tight, too, everyone would be able to see my goose-pimples, but on the whole I was pleased with the result – it was definitely one of my on days. The only problem was that when I put on my new tights, the crotch only came up to the middle of my thighs. I gave them a tug and they split irrevocably, leaving a large hole, so I had to make do with bare legs.

I was just trying to give myself a better cleavage with Sellotape when Rory announced that he was ready. Even I, though, was unprepared for his beauty, dressed up in a dark green velvet doublet with white lace at the throat and wrists and the dark green and blue kilt of the Balniels. Pale and haughty, his eyes glittering with bad temper, he looked like something out of *Kidnapped*; Alan Breck Stuart or young Lochinvar coming out of the West.

'Oh,' I sighed. 'You do look lovely.'

Rory grimaced and tugged at the frills at his neck.

'I feel like Kenneth McKellar,' he said.

'Never mind, you've got exactly the right hips to wear a pleated skirt,' I said.

Rory put a long tartan muffler thing on the dressing-table. 'This is for you,' he said.

'I'm not thinking of going out in this weather,' I said.

'You wear it indoors,' he said, draping it diagonally across my shoulders, 'like this, and pin it here.'

'But whatever for?' I moaned.

'It's the Balniel tartan,' he said evenly. 'Married women are supposed to wear their husband's tartan.'

'But it completely covers up my cleavage.'

'Just as well, you're not at some orgy in Chelsea now,' said Rory.

'Do I really have to, it's a bit Hooray for me.'

Very sulkily I arranged it; somehow tartan didn't go with skintight pink satin, and brooches on the navel.

I wanted to fiddle with my hair and make-up a few minutes longer, but Rory was sitting on the bed, staring at me coldly, making me nervous.

'Why don't you go on down?' I said.

'I'll wait here,' he said.

I combed a few pink tendrils over my shoulders.

'What made you go crazy with the cochineal?' said Rory.

'I thought I ought to change my image,' I said, sourly. 'My old one didn't seem to be getting me very far.'

Downstairs in the huge drawing-room people were having drinks. The host and hostess stood near the door repeating the same words of welcome to new arrivals. Looking round I realized I looked better than most of the women but infinitely more tarty. Most of them were big, raw-boned deb types in very covered-up clothes, the occasional mottled purple arms were the nearest they got to *décolletage*. Very tall, aristocratic men in kilts stood talking in haw haw voices about getting their lochs drained and burning their grouse moors. Fishes in glass cases and mounted stags' heads stared glassily down from the walls.

Fiona and Charles were standing near the door. She was wearing a blue dress and absolutely no eye make-up.

'What a pretty dress,' I said, with desperate insincerity.

'Yes, everyone likes it,' she said, 'blue is Charles' favourite colour.'

Charles was gaping at my pink hair, his mouth even more open than usual. Fiona started trying to bring Rory out about his painting.

'Do you do all that funny abstract stuff?' she said.

'No,' said Rory.

'Some young man – he had a beard actually – painted my sister Sarah. She sat for two hours and all he had drawn after all that time were three figs and a milk bottle.'

She gave a tinkle of laughter, Rory looked at her stonily.

'Charles paints quite beautifully too, I feel it's such a shame his job in the City is so demanding he doesn't have time to take painting up as a hobby – like you, Rory.'

'Rory *does not paint* as a hobby,' I said furiously, 'it's his profession.' But I spoke to deaf ears, Rory had turned on his heel and gone off to get himself a drink. Charles and Fiona were suddenly shrieking at a couple who had just come into the room.

I was extremely pleased therefore that the next moment Calen Macdonald bore down on me and kissed first my hand, then my cheek, then both my bare shoulders.

'I was just saying to Buster I wished I could see more of you,' he said, pulling down my tartan sash and peering at my cleavage, 'and now I have. I must say that dress is very fetching, pink looks like bare flesh if one shuts one's eyes.'

'Where's Deidre?' I said.

'Oh, she's stalking in Inverness.'

I giggled.

'So I've got the whole evening off and I'm going to devote it entirely to you.'

Two matrons with red-veined faces stopped discussing herbaceous borders and looked at us frostily.

At that moment a voice shouted 'Emily!' and there was Coco, dripping with sapphires as big as gull's eggs, wearing a glorious midnight blue dress. She was lying like Madame Recamier on a red brocade sofa, surrounded by admirers.

Rory sat at her feet.

'I didn't see you,' I said, going over and kissing her.

'You look very nice, doesn't she, Rory,' said Coco.

'A bit prawn cocktail,' said Rory.

I bit my lip.

'I think she looks tremendous,' said Buster giving me a warm look. 'In the pink, I might say,' he laughed heartily.

The room was filling up. Buster and Calen were joined by some ancient general, and they were soon busy recounting to each other the number of creatures they had slaughtered in the last week.

'Grouses, and twelve bores, and twenty bores, and million bores, that's all men can think about up here,' said Coco. She began talking to me about shoes.

There was a sudden stir and a whisper ran through the room. The old general straightened his tie and smoothed his moustache.

'What a beautiful girl,' he said.

A swift flush mounted to Rory's pale cheeks. With a sinking heart, without turning my head, I knew it must be Marina.

'Hello, everyone,' she said, coming over and kissing Coco, 'how's your poor leg, darling?'

She was wearing a pale grey chiffon dress, smothered in two huge pale grey feather boas. With her flaming red hair it made one think of beech woods in autumn against a cloudy sky. I noticed she had no truck with Hamish's tartan across her bosom. I supposed it was Rory's tartan she was after. Sadly I realized that if I spent a million years on my face and clothes, I would never be as beautiful as Marina. Hamish, all done up in black velvet and frills, looked awful.

'Mutton dressed as cutlet,' said Rory to Marina under his breath. Even worse was to come. Following her into the room came Finn Maclean in a dinner jacket, with a sleek brunette.

'Oh God,' said Rory, 'here comes the virgin surgeon. Diney,' he added, turning to the daughter of the house, 'what the hell is Doctor Finlay doing here?'

'He was absolutely wonderful about Mummy's ulcer,' said Diney, her eyes shining.

'Probably gave it to her in the first place,' said Rory.

'Well, I must say, I think he's rather super myself,' said Diney.

'I'm surprised at you,' said Rory, 'one really shouldn't know one's doctor socially.'

Finn came up to Coco.

'How's it feeling?' he said.

'Much better,' said Coco.

'May be, but there must be no dancing on it,' he said firmly.

'Who's that with him?' I whispered to Calen Macdonald.

'I think she's one of his nurses,' said Calen.

'She's pretty,' I said.

'Not my type,' said Calen, and started whispering sweet everythings into my ear. I, however, was much more interested in seeing how Rory and Finn reacted to each other.

'Look, Rory,' said Coco, 'here's Finn.'

Rory, just lighting a cigarette, paused, eyeing Finn without any friendliness.

Finn nodded coldly, 'Hello, Rory,' he said.

'Good evening, Doctor,' said Rory – he smiled but

his eyes were cold, his face as pale as marble. There was an awkward pause.

'Isn't it nice Finn's back for good,' said Coco brightly to the assembled company.

'Not for my good, he isn't,' said Rory.

'This is Frances,' said Finn, ignoring him and introducing the sleek brunette. 'She works at the hospital.'

'Oh, a staff outing,' drawled Rory, 'what fun. Did you come here by charabanc with a crate of beer, or is it part of the S.R.N. syllabus – a dazzling night of dancing and passion in the arms of Doctor Maclean?'

'Only for very privileged nurses,' said Frances, smiling at Finn.

'I'm surprised you've been able to drag him away from delivering babies and darning up appendices,' said Rory.

Frances was obviously uncertain how to take Rory.

'Dr Maclean certainly doesn't allow himself enough free time,' she said warmly.

'Quite so,' said Rory, his eyes lighting up with malicious amusement. 'He's an example to us all. I gather that's the reason your marriage came unstuck, Finn. I heard your ex-wife couldn't cope with the short hours, or wasn't your double bed-side manner up to scratch? However,' he smiled at Frances, 'you seem to be consoling yourself very nicely.'

I turned away in embarrassment; if only he wouldn't be so poisonous. Rory grabbed my arm.

'You haven't met Emily, have you, Finn?'

'Yes he has,' I said quickly.

'Oh?' Rory raised an eyebrow.

'We met at Coco's one day,' I said, 'when Finn came to see her about her ankle.' Rory held out his glass to a passing waiter to fill up.

'Are you still trying to paint?' Finn said.

'He's got an exhibition in London in April,' I said hotly.

'Doesn't really need one,' said Finn. 'He's been making an exhibition of himself for years,' and taking Frances by the arm, crossed the room to talk to his host.

'Scintillating as ever,' said Rory, but his hand shook as he lit one cigarette from another.

'Do you like dancing reels, Emily?' said Marina.

'If I have enough to drink,' I said, draining my glass, 'I reel automatically.'

We went in to dinner.

The leathery, sneering faces of ancestors looked down from the walls. The candlelight flickered on the gleaming panelling, the suits of armour, the long polished table with its shining silver and glasses, and on the pearly white shoulders of Marina.

'I hope there's a huge flower arrangement in front of me so I don't have to sit staring at Doctor Maclean,' said Rory.

I was horrified to see that he and Marina were

sitting next to each other on the opposite side of the table. I was next to Calen, who ran his fingers all over my bare back when he pushed my chair in. And now the bad news. On my other side was six feet four inches of Titian-haired disapproval – Finn Maclean.

'Hello, Finn,' said Calen, 'how are things, have you met this steaming girl?'

'Doctor Maclean isn't one of my fans,' I said.

'Maybe not,' said Calen, 'but he's tall enough to see right down your front, unless I rearrange that sash. That's better, don't want to give you blood pressure, do we Finn? Always get swollen heads, these quacks, think all the nurses and women patients are nuts about them.'

I laughed, Finn didn't.

'It must be exciting, running your own hospital,' I said to him. He was about to answer when someone shoved a steaming great soup ladle between us. 'Great fun running your own hospital,' I went on. Then it was his turn to help himself to soup.

'What's the disease people suffer most often from round here?' I asked.

'Verbal diarrhoea,' muttered Calen.

I was just warming to my subject, asking Finn all the right questions about the hospital and the operations he would perform there, when Calen lifted up the curtain of hair hanging over my left ear and whispered: 'Christ, I want to take you to bed.'

I started to laugh in mid-sentence, then blushed:

'I'm awfully sorry,' I said to Finn, 'it's just something Calen said.'

Finn obviously thought we were too silly for words and turned his huge back on me and started talking to the girl on his right.

Footmen moved round the table, the clatter of plates mingled with the clink of knives and glasses and the hum of various animated conversations. Lady Downleesh sat at the end of the table, a large imposing woman who must once have been handsome. Only Marina and Rory sat mutely side by side, talking little, eating less. They appeared to see and hear nothing of what was going on around them. Suddenly I felt panicky. They were probably playing footy-footy. I imagined their cloven hoofs entwined. Calen and Finn were temporarily occupied with other conversations. I dropped my napkin and dived under the table to retrieve it. It was very dark. I hoped my eyes would soon become accustomed to it, but they didn't; not enough carrots when I was a child I suppose. I couldn't see which were Rory's or Marina's legs. I grabbed someone's ankle, but it was much too fat for Marina's and twitched convulsively – cheap thrill!!! All the same, I couldn't stay here for ever exciting dowagers. I surfaced again.

'Are you all right, Mrs Balniel?' said Lady Downleesh, looking somewhat startled.

'Fine,' I squeaked, 'absolutely marvellous soup.'

'Everyone's waiting for you to finish yours,' said Finn in an undertone.

'Oh I have,' I said, 'I've got a tiny appetite, I never eat between males.'

Finn didn't laugh. Pompous old stuffed shirt.

Everyone started to talk about fishing as the soup plates were moved.

'You're not a bit alike,' I said, 'you and Marina.'

He shot me a wary glance.

'In what way?'

'Well, she's so wild and you're so well controlled. I can't see you as a medical student putting stuffed gorillas in college scarves down Matron's bed.'

He gave me one of those big on-off smiles he must use all the time for keeping people at a polite distance.

'I was working too hard for that.'

'Are all the people in this room your patients?' I asked. 'Must be funny to look round a table and know what every single woman looks like with her clothes off.'

'Calen does anyway,' said Finn. 'What do you do with yourself all day?'

'Not a lot, I'm not very good at housework. I read and grumble, sometimes I even bite my nails.'

'You ought to get a job, give you something to do,' he went on. 'What did you do before you met Rory?'

'Oh, I mistyped letters in several offices, and I did a bit of modelling when I got thin enough, and then I got engaged to an M.P. I don't think I would have been much of an asset to him, and then Rory came along.'

'It's a full moon tonight,' said a horse-faced blonde sitting opposite us. 'I wonder if the ghost'll walk tonight. Who's sleeping in the west wing?'

'The Frayns,' said Diney Downleesh, lowering her voice, 'and Rory and his new wife.'

'What ghost?' I whispered nervously to Calen.

Calen laughed. 'Oh, it's nothing. There was a Downleesh younger son a couple of centuries ago, who fell in love with his elder brother's wife. The wife evidently had a soft spot for him as well. One night, when her husband was away, she invited the younger brother into her bedroom. He was just hot-footing along the West Tower where she was sleeping (all tarted up in his white dressing-gown), when the husband came back, and picking a dirk off the wall, he stabbed him. The younger brother is supposed to stalk the passage when there's a full moon, trying to avenge himself through all eternity for not getting his oats.'

'How creepy,' I said with a shiver.

'I'll take care of you,' said Calen, putting his hand on my thigh and encountering bare flesh.

'Christ,' he said.

'My only pair of tights split,' I said.

Finn Maclean pretended not to notice. Calen filled my glass over and over again.

Eventually we finished dinner and the ball began. The host and hostess stood at the edge of the long gallery welcoming latecomers. Every time the front door opened you could feel a blast of icy air from outside. It was terribly cold in these big houses. The only way to keep warm was to stand near one of the huge log fires that were burning in each room, then two minutes later you were bright scarlet in the face. I could see exactly why Burns said his love was like a red, red rose.

Rory came up to me. 'What was Finn Maclean talking to you about?' he said suspiciously.

'He was stressing the importance of getting one's teeth into something,' I said.

'If he got his teeth into me, I'd go straight off and have a rabies jab,' said Rory.

'On with the dance,' I said. 'Let Emily be unconfined.'

'Come on, Rory,' said Diney Downleesh, coming over to us, 'we need two more people to make up an eightsome over there.'

We couldn't really refuse.

Dum-diddy Dum-diddy Dum-diddy-diddy-diddy went the accordions. The men gave strange, unearthly wails, like a train not stopping at a station. We circled to the left, we circled to the right.

'Wrong way,' hissed Rory, as we swung into the grand chain. When it was my turn in the middle, I made an even worse hash of it, setting to all the wrong people and doing U-turns instead of figures of eight, and whooping a lot. 'For Christ's sake stop capering around like the White Heather Club,' said Rory under his breath. 'Women don't put their hands up, or click their fingers, or whoop.'

The next dance, thank God, was an ordinary one. I danced it with Buster, who squeezed me so hard, I thought I'd shoot out of my dress like toothpaste.

'Why don't any of them look as though they're enjoying themselves?' I said.

'You can never tell until they fall on the floor,' said Buster.

On the other side of the room Marina was dancing with Hamish. She looked so glowingly beautiful and he so yellow and old and decayed I was suddenly reminded of Mary Queen of Scots dancing and dancing her ancient husband into the grave.

The evening wore on. I wasn't short of partners. I danced every dance.

A piper came on, well primed with whisky, and assaulted our ear-drums for a couple of reels. My reputation as a reel-wrecker was growing. I messed up Hamilton House and then the Duke and Duchess of Perth, and then the Sixteensome. On the surface I must have appeared rather like a loose horse in the National, potentially dangerous, thoroughly enjoying myself and quite out of control. But through a haze of alcohol and misery I was aware of two things, Rory's complete indifference to my behaviour and Finn Maclean's disapproval. Both made me behave even worse.

I danced a great deal with Calen. I came into my own when they stopped doing those silly reels.

'Did your wife dance professionally?' I heard a disapproving dowager say to Rory, as I came off the floor after a gruelling Charleston. Calen and I went into the drawing-room for yet another drink. I put my glass down on a gleaming walnut table. When I picked it up two minutes later, there was a large ring on the table.

'Oh God,' I said, 'how awful.'

'Looks better that way,' said Calen, 'looks more lived in somehow.' He led me back on to the floor. The music was slow and dreamy now.

'You are the promised breath of springtime,' sang Calen laying his handsome face against mine. I snuggled up against him for a few laps round the floor, and then I escaped to the loo. Big-boned girls stood around talking about Harrods and their coming-out dances. Really, I thought as I gazed in the mirror, I look very loose indeed. Tight dress, loose morals, I suppose.

I wandered along the long gallery so I could watch the people on the floor. A double line of dancers were engaged with serious faces in executing a reel. Marina and Rory faced one another, expressionless. God they danced beautifully. I was reminded of Lochinvar again:

> So stately his form and so lovely her face
> That never a hall such a galliard did grace . . .
> And the bride's maidens whispered, 'T'were
>   better by far
> To have matched our fair cousin with young
>   Lochinvar.

Oh dear, I thought in misery. In this case young Lochinvar seems to have missed the boat, arriving too late and finding his love married to Hamish.

The dance ended. The couples clapped and spilled out into the hall. If only Rory would come and look for me. But it looked as though I'd have to wait for a Ladies' Excuse Me before I had a chance to dance with him again.

I heard footsteps behind me. I felt two hands go round my waist, I turned hopefully, but it was Calen.

'I've got a bottle,' he said, 'let's go and drink it somewhere more secluded.' He dropped a kiss on to my shoulder and led me downstairs along a long passage into a conservatory.

Chinese lanterns, hanging round the walls, lit up the huge tropical plants. The scent of azaleas, hyacinths and white chrysanthemums mingled voluptuously with the Arpège I'd poured all over myself. The sound of the band reached us faintly from the hall.

'You are the promised breath of springtime,' sang Calen, taking me in his arms.

'There isn't any mistletoe,' I said.

'We don't need it,' said Calen, his grey, dissipated eyes gazing into mine.

You're rotten to the core, I thought. Mad, bad and dangerous to know. Bad from the neck upwards, and not at all good for Emily. Not that Rory was doing much good for me either.

'God, I want you,' said Calen undoing the top

button of my dress. He bent his head and kissed the top of my cleavage, and slowly kissed his way up my neck and chin to my mouth.

I didn't feel anything really, except a desire to slake my loneliness. God, it was a practised kiss. I thought of all those hundreds of women he must have seduced. Hands travelled over my bare back, pressing into every crevice. Suddenly a light flicked on in the library next door.

'Calen,' said a voice, 'you're wanted on the telephone.'

'Go to hell,' said Calen, burying his face in my neck, 'don't be a bloody spoilsport, Finn.'

Over Calen's head, our eyes met. 'It's Deidre,' Finn said.

'Oh God,' sighed Calen, as reluctantly he let me go. 'You see before you the most henpecked husband in the Highlands. Goodnight, you dream of bliss.' He kissed me on the cheek and walked somewhat unsteadily out of the conservatory. Finn and I glared at each other.

'You are beyond the pale,' I snapped, 'beyond a whole dairyful of pales. Why do you have to rush around rotting up people's sex lives? I thought you were a doctor, not a vicar.' I lurched slightly without Calen to hold me up.

'You won't get Rory back that way,' said Finn. 'Getting drunk and going to bed with Calen doesn't solve anything.'

'Oh it does, it does,' I said with a sigh, 'it gets you

through the next half an hour — and half an hour can be an eternity in Scotland.'

I wandered into the library and discovered a glass of champagne balanced on a stag's head. I drank it in one gulp.

'I'll take the high road and ye'll take the low road,' I said, 'and I'll be inebriated before ye. Tell me, Doctor, you know the area better than I do, what gives between Rory and your sister?'

'Nothing,' he said roughly. 'You're imagining things, and you're not making things any better behaving like this.'

I stared at him for a minute. 'My mother once had an English setter who had freckles like yours,' I said, dreamily. 'They looked really nice on a dog.'

We went into the hall which was fortunately deserted. 'What about your friend Frances Nightingale,' I said, swinging back and forth on an heraldic leopard that reared up the bottom of the banisters. 'Isn't she missing you?'

'That's my problem,' he said.

'Look,' I said, 'I'm not usually as silly as this. It's a pity you're not as good at mending broken hearts as broken bones.'

'I suggest,' said Finn, 'you go straight up to bed without making a fool of yourself any further. Take three Alka-Seltzers before you go to sleep, you'll feel much better in the morning. Come on.' He moved forward to take me upstairs, but I broke away.

'Go and jump in the loch,' I snarled, and ran away from him up the stairs. I fell into bed, preparing to cry myself to sleep, but I must have flaked out almost immediately.

In the middle of the night, it seemed, I woke up. I didn't know where I was, it was pitch black in the room. The fire had gone out. Where the hell was I? Then I remembered – Downleesh Castle. I put out a hand – groping for Rory. He wasn't there, I was alone in the huge four-poster. Suddenly the room seemed to go unnaturally cold, the wind was blowing a blizzard outside, the snow still falling heavily. As the windows rattled and banged and the doors and stairs creaked, it was like being on board ship. Then I felt my hair standing on end as I remembered the ghost in the white dressing-gown that walked when the moon was full. I gave a sob at the thought of him creeping down those long, musty passages towards me. I was trembling all over. Getting out of bed, I ran my hands along the wall, hysterically groping for a light switch. I couldn't find one. The room grew even colder. Suddenly I gave a gasp of terror as the curtain blew in, and I realized to my horror the window was open. I leapt back into bed. Where the hell was Rory? How could he leave me like this? Suddenly my blood froze as, very, very gently, I heard the door creaking. It stopped, then creaked again, and, very, very gradually, it began to open. I couldn't move, my voice was strangled in my dry throat, my heart pounding.

Oh God, I croaked, oh, please no! I tried desperately to scream as one does in a nightmare, but no sound came out.

Slowly the door opened wider. The curtains billowed again in the through draught from the window, and the light from the snow revealed a ghostly figure wrapped in white, gold hair gleaming. It suddenly turned and looked in my direction, and slowly crept towards the bed. Panic overwhelmed me, I was going to be murdered.

Someone was screaming horribly, echoing on and on through the house. The next minute I realized it was me. The room was flooded with light and there was Buster, standing in the doorway, looking very discomfited in a white silk dressing-gown. I went on screaming.

'Emily, my God,' said Buster. 'I'm so sorry, pet. For Christ's sake stop making that frightful row. I got into the wrong bedroom, must have got the wrong wing for that matter.'

I stopped screaming and burst into noisy, hysterical sobs. Next minute Finn Maclean barged in, still wearing black trousers and his white evening shirt.

'What the hell's going on?' he said.

He was followed by the Frayns. She had tied her hair up with a blue bow.

'Where's Rory?' I sobbed, 'where *is* he? I'm sorry, Buster, I thought you were the ghost. I was so frightened.' My breath was coming in great strangled gasps. Buster patted my shoulder gingerly.

'There, there, poor Emily,' he said. 'Got my wings muddled,' he added to Finn. 'She thought I was the Downleesh ghost.'

'I'm not surprised after all the liquor she shipped,' said Finn. 'I'll go and get something to calm her down.'

Once I started crying I couldn't stop.

'Do try and pull yourself together, Emily,' said Fiona. 'Oughtn't you to slap her face or something?' she said as Finn came back with a couple of pills and a glass of water.

'Get these down you,' he said, gently.

'I don't need them,' I sobbed, then gave another scream as Rory walked in through the curtains, snowflakes thick on his hair and his shoulders.

'What a lot of people in my wife's bedroom,' he said blandly, looking round the room. 'I didn't know you were entertaining, Emily. You do keep extra-ordinary hours.' A muscle was going in his cheek, he looked ghastly.

'Where have you been?' I said, trying and failing to stop crying.

'Having a quiet cigarette on the battlements,' said Rory. 'Pondering whether there was life after birth. Hello, Buster, I didn't see you, how nice of you to drop in on Emily. Does my mother know you're here?'

'She was quite hysterical,' said Fiona, reprovingly.

'I'm not surprised,' said Rory, 'with all these people in here.' He came over and patted me on the shoulder. 'There, there, lovie, pack it in now, everything's all right.'

'I thought Buster was a ghost,' I explained, feeling terribly silly. 'I could only see his dressing-gown and his hair.'

'You what?' For a minute Rory looked at Buster incredulously, and then he leant against the wall and started to shake with laughter.

'I got into the wrong wing,' said Buster, looking very discomfited. 'Perfectly natural mistake in these old houses, thought I was going into my own bedroom.'

Rory sniffed, still laughing. 'I didn't know ghosts reeked of aftershave. Really, Buster, next time you go bed-hopping, you should take an A–Z. Just think if you ended up in our hostess's room.' He looked round the room. 'Well, if you've all finished, I'd quite like to go to bed.'

Finn Maclean glared at Rory for a second and then stalked out of the room, followed by Buster followed by the Frayns.

'What an extraordinary couple,' I could hear her saying, 'do you think they could be a bit mad?'

Still laughing, Rory started pulling off his tie. There was a knock on the door.

'Probably Buster wondering if he's forgotten someone,' said Rory. Sure enough, Buster stood on the threshold. 'Rory, dear boy, just like a word with you.'

'Knowing you, it'll be several words,' said Rory.

'Don't say anything to your mother about this, will you?' I heard Buster saying in a low voice. 'She's been under a lot of strain with her ankle, just taken a sleeping pill, wouldn't want to upset her.'

'You're an old goat, Buster,' said Rory. 'But your secret is safe with Emily and me. I can't, alas, vouch for Doctor Maclean, who is the soul of indiscretion, or for that appalling couple we gave a lift to.'

'Goodness,' I said after he'd gone. 'Do you think he was being unfaithful to Coco?'

'Probably,' said Rory. 'He and my mother trust each other just about as far as they can throw each other, which always seems a good basis for marriage.'

'But whose bedroom was he trying to get into?' I asked.

'Probably taking pot-luck,' said Rory.

'Marina's perhaps,' I said, then could have bitten my tongue off.

'Marina left hours ago, she and Hamish aren't staying here,' said Rory. 'They were having the most frightful row when they left. They should lay off arguing occasionally, a short rest would re-charge their batteries for starting again.'

So he hadn't been with Marina. Instead he'd been on the battlements by himself in a blizzard, driven by what extremes of despair. Somehow that seemed even worse. He got into bed, put his arms round me and kissed me on the forehead. I could never understand his changes of mood.

'Sorry you were frightened by Buster,' he said, and the next moment he was asleep. I lay awake for a long time. Towards dawn he rolled over and caught hold of me, groaning, 'Oh my darling, my little love.' I realized he was asleep and, with a sick agony, that it certainly wasn't me he was talking to.

Chapter Fifteen

For the first time I dreaded Christmas. At home it had been our own, cosy, womb-like festival, but with Rory there wasn't likely to be peace on earth, or goodwill towards men. Half-heartedly I chose a fir tree from the plantation behind our house and set it in a tub, put holly on the walls, strung a bit of mistletoe from the drawing-room light.

On Christmas Eve I went into Penlorren to do last-minute shopping and buy some little presents for Rory's stocking. I left Rory cleaning his gun for the shoot Buster had arranged for Boxing Day.

When I got back, weighed down with parcels, there was a car parked outside the gate. I let myself in and was just about to shout I was back, when I heard raised voices from the studio. I tiptoed closer so I could distinguish them. One was like rough sand with a pronounced Scottish accent, the other aristo-cratic, drawling, silken with menace. Through the door I could see Finn and Rory facing each other, like a huge lion and a sleek, slim, black panther, obviously in the middle of a blazing row. Neither of them heard me.

'Well, Doctor?' said Rory, the words dripping with insolence. 'Why are you hounding me like this?'

'Because I've got several things I want to say to you.'

'Well, don't say them now. Emily'll be back any moment.'

'I don't know what devilish game you're up to this time,' said Finn, 'but you'd better stop playing cat and mouse with my sister. Leave her alone, you've done enough damage.'

I felt my throat go dry. I held on to the door handle for support.

'Marina's over twenty-one. Surely she's old enough to take care of herself,' said Rory.

'You know she can't,' thundered Finn. 'You of all people must know how near the edge she is. Don't you ever think of Hamish?'

'Not if I can help it,' said Rory in a bored voice.

'Or Emily?'

'Leave Emily out of it. She's my problem. You should really visit us more often, Finn. You're like a breath of fresh air.'

'You damned little rat,' roared Finn. 'You're going to carry on as before, aren't you?'

'Well, things are slightly more complicated now, but on the whole, Doctor, you've got a pretty clear view of things.'

'You know I can put the police on you, don't you?' said Finn.

Suddenly Rory lost his temper. He went as white as a sheet, his black eyes blazed.

'You wouldn't dare,' he hissed. 'Your family would come out of it as badly as mine.'

'I don't care.'

Their faces were almost touching in their rage.

Then Rory's control seemed to desert him. He sprang at Finn, howling abuse, his fingers round Finn's throat. At one moment it seemed as though Finn was going to be murdered. The next, Rory had gone down before a crashing blow on the jaw, and Finn was standing over him, fists clenched, about to kick Rory's head in.

'No!' I screamed. 'No! Don't touch him.'

Finn swung round, his yellow eyes blazing. Then he looked down at Rory.

'That's only the beginning, Rory,' he said. 'I won't be so gentle with you next time.'

And he was gone.

'Are you all right?' I said.

'Fine,' Rory said. 'I do love Christmas, don't you? It brings out those delightful histrionic qualities latent in all of us.'

I didn't laugh.

'I suppose you're going to tell me he was talking nonsense,' I said, 'that there wasn't any truth in his accusations.'

Rory poured himself a drink and downed it in

one, then he banged the glass down.

'What do you think, Emily? That's what matters.'

'I don't think anything,' I said, biting my lip to stop myself crying. 'I just know you haven't made love to me for nearly three months and it's driving me crazy. Then Finn comes here and says all these things, and they seem to add up.'

Rory picked up the gun from the table and examined it. 'So, you're not getting your ration,' he said softly.

'Put that thing away,' I said nervously.

'Does it frighten you? Poor, frustrated Emily.'

He lifted the gun, his finger on the trigger.

'Don't!' I screamed.

He aimed the gun upwards. There was a muted explosion, the crash of a light bulb, and the studio was in darkness. The next minute a wedge of muscle and flesh hurled itself against me, knocking the breath out of my body, pinioning me to the carpet. Then Rory's mouth ground against mine with such intensity our teeth clashed. I struggled helplessly like a fly against a wall, trying to push him away.

'No, Rory, no,' I shrieked.

'You wanted it,' he swore. 'You're bloody well going to get it.'

It was over in a few seconds. I lay on the floor, rocking from side to side, my hands over my mouth. My ribs felt as though they'd crack with agony from the dry sobs I couldn't utter.

Rory flicked on the side light and shone it in my face.

'That's what you wanted, wasn't it? You don't seem pleased.'

I gazed at him dumbly, I could feel the tears welling out of my eyes.

'You hate my guts, don't you?' I whispered.

'It's your lack of guts I hate,' he said.

Then, suddenly, he put his arms round me and pulled me against him. I jerked my head away.

'Oh, Emily, Emily,' he muttered, 'I'm so miserable, and I've made you miserable, too. Forgive me, I don't know what gets into me.'

Running a dry tongue over my lips and tasting the blood congealing there, I digested this outburst. I should have tried to comfort him, to find out what drove him to these black, uncontrollable rages. But I didn't feel up to it. Without a word, I shook him off, got to my feet, and walked out of the room, banging the door shut.

Chapter Sixteen

Looking back on a time of intense unhappiness, one fortunately remembers very little. Our marriage was into injury time. Somehow we got through Christmas and the next month; hardly speaking, licking our wounds, yet still putting up a front to the outside world. Over and over I made plans to leave, but could never quite bring myself to. In spite of everything I still loved Rory.

February brought snow, turning the island into a place of magic.

Coco's ankle recovered and she decided to give a birthday party for Buster.

Rory went to Glasgow for the night to stock up with paint, but was due back at lunchtime on the day of the party.

I went to sleep and had the most terrible nightmare about Marina and Rory, lying tangled in each other's arms, asleep on the floor. I woke up in floods of tears, with the moon in my eyes and the screaming horrors in my mind. I groped for Rory beside me, and then remembered he wasn't there. I was too frightened to go back to sleep again. I got up and cleaned the house from top to toe (my charwoman had been off for several weeks with rheumatism), and spent hours cooking Rory a gorgeous lunch to welcome him home. Then I went out and bought two bottles of really good wine. From now on I decided I was going to make a last effort to save my marriage.

At twelve o'clock the telephone rang. It was Rory. He was still in Edinburgh. He'd be back later, in time for Coco's party.

'Why bother to come back home at all?' I said, and slammed down the telephone, all my good resolutions gone to pot. How the hell was I to fill in the time until he got back? I refused to cry. I decided to drive into Penlorren and buy Buster a present.

Two miles from home I suddenly realized I'd come out without my purse, and decided to turn round and get it. The road was icy and inches deep in snow. My U-turn was disastrously unsuccessful. The next thing I was stuck across the road, the wheels whirring up snow every time I pressed the accelerator.

Suddenly, around the corner, a dark blue car came thundering towards me, going much too fast even without ice on the roads. I screamed with terror but was absolutely powerless to move. There was no way it could brake in time. Then by some miracle of steering, the driver managed to yank the car to the right, slithering into a sixteen-yard skid, missing my car by inches, before juddering to a halt in a snowdrift.

Trust my luck. It was my old enemy Finn Maclean who got out of the car, all red hair and lowered black brows, jaw corners and narrow, infuriated eyes. 'What the blazes do you think . . .' he began, then he realized it was me, took a deep breath and said, 'God, I might have known.'

He looked me over in a way that made me feel very small, and hot and uncomfortable.

'I couldn't help it,' I blurted out, still shaking from shock.

'That's what I'm complaining about,' he said wearily. 'I'm sure you couldn't help it; only an imbecile would have attempted to turn a car around here.'

'I've said I'm sorry,' I said, colouring hotly. 'Anyway, you were driving much too fast and my car skidded. No-one could have moved it.'

'Get out,' said Finn brusquely.

I got out. He got in and turned the car immediately. Then he got out and held the door open for me.

'Nothing to it,' he said, infuriatingly. 'You were just using too much choke.'

It was the last straw. I got into the car, just looked at him and burst into tears; then, crashing the gears, I roared off home. God knows how I got back with the whole countryside swimming with tears.

I don't know how long I cried, but long enough to make me look as ugly as sin. Then I noticed the potted plant Coco had given me for Christmas. It looked limp and dejected.

'Needs a bit of love and attention, like me,' I said dismally, and getting up, I got a watering can and gave it some water.

Then I remembered someone had once told me if you watered rush mats it brought out the green. I heard a step. I must have left the door open. Hoping by some miracle it might be Rory, I looked up. It was Finn Maclean.

'Don't you come cat-footing in here,' I snarled.

Then I realized how stupid it must look, me standing there watering carpets in the middle of the drawing-room.

'I'm not quite off my rocker,' I said weakly. 'It's meant to bring out the green in the rushes.'

Finn began to laugh.

'Whenever I see you you're either tearing up roses with your teeth, trying to block the traffic, or watering carpets. How come you're such a nutcase?'

'I don't know,' I muttered. 'I think I was dropped as an adult.'

'You're going to water the whole floor in a minute,' he said, taking the watering can away from me.

For a minute he looked at me consideringly. Aware how puffy and red my eyes were, I gazed at my feet.

Then he said, 'I came to apologize for biting your head off this morning. I was tired, I hadn't been to bed. Still, it was no excuse, and I'm sorry.'

I was so surprised I sat down on the sofa.

'That's all right,' I said, 'I had a lousy night too, otherwise I wouldn't have cried.'

'Where's Rory?'

'In Glasgow.'

'I'm going over to Mullin this afternoon to see a patient, why don't you come too?'

'I get sick on planes,' I said quickly.

'You can't land a plane there. I'm taking the speedboat. I'll pick you up in half an hour. We needn't talk if we don't want to.'

Chapter Seventeen

It was a beautiful day: the sun shone and the hills glittered like mountains of salt against an arctic blue sky. The gloom was still on me as we ploughed over the dark green water, but I found it easier to endure, particularly when I found Finn and I could talk or not talk, with a reasonable amount of ease. When we moored and I leapt on to the landing-stage, he caught me, and his hands were steady and reassuring like a man used to handling women.

As we walked up the mountainside to a little grey farmhouse, the bracken glittered white like ostrich feathers of purest glass, snow sparkled an inch on every leaf, icicles hung four feet deep. Suddenly, an old woman, her arm in plaster, came running out of an outhouse beside the farm.

'Doctor!' she screamed, 'thank God ye've come, it's me wee cow.'

'Careful, you'll slip,' said Finn, taking her good arm.

'What's the matter with her?'

'She's started calving and things dinna look too

well. Angus went to the mainland for help, but he's not back yet.'

'I'll have a look at her,' said Finn, going into the outhouse.

A terrified, moaning, threshing cow was lying in the corner.

'Easy now,' said Finn soothingly, and went up to her. He had a look then called, 'She's pretty far gone, Bridget.'

The old woman promptly started crying and wailing that it was their only cow.

'Go back to the house,' Finn told her, 'I'll do what I can. You'll only be a hindrance with that arm. Come on,' he added to me, 'you can help.'

'I can't,' I squeaked. 'I don't know anything about cows. Shall I take the boat back to the island and get help?'

'It's too late,' said Finn, rolling up his sleeves. As he spoke, the cow gave another terrified moan of pain.

'Oh, all right,' I said sulkily. 'Tell me what to do.'

'Hold on to the calf's legs,' said Finn, 'and when I say "pull", pull hard.'

'Gawd,' I muttered. 'What a way to spend a Thursday.'

The straw was already sticky with blood and there was only one 30-watt bulb to work under. Finn barked out instructions.

'Haven't you got any Pethedine for her?' I said.

Finn didn't answer. I supposed he was used to

delivering babies. But women in labour don't usually flail and lurch around like cows do.

'I'm sure she'd be less uptight if the bull had been present at the birth,' I joked weakly, as I picked myself up from the stinking straw for the third time.

After that I stopped making jokes, but just gritted my teeth and followed Finn's instructions, aware that despite his Herculean strength, he could be surprisingly gentle. Then, at last, a thin, long-legged calf was lying safe on the straw, being proudly licked by its mother.

'Oh, isn't it sweet?' I said, tears pricking my eyelids.

'Well done,' said Finn. I felt as though he'd given me the Nobel Prize. 'Come inside and have a wash. Bridget'll give us a cup of tea.'

On the boat home he said, 'You look absolutely whacked.'

'It isn't often I spend the afternoon playing mid-wife to a cow,' I said.

'Come along to the surgery tomorrow,' he said. 'I'd like to have a look at you.'

I blushed, absurdly flattered at his concern.

'How's the hospital going?' I asked.

'Fine. Three wards completed already.'

'You must be run off your feet.'

He shrugged his shoulders. 'I've got a new intern starting next week which'll help.'

'What's he like?'

'It's a she.'

'Oh,' I said, momentarily nonplussed. 'What's she like?'

'Very attractive. I chose her myself.'

'For yourself?'

'Bit early to tell. I'm a romantic, I suppose. All part of the Celtic hang-up. I don't think the man-woman thing should be conducted on a rabbit level.'

The lights were coming on in Penlorren now, pale in the fading light. I felt stupidly displeased at the thought of some glamorous woman doctor working with Finn. I saw her with slim ankles, and not a hair out of place, white coat open to show an ample cashmere bosom.

'What happened to your marriage?' I asked.

'My wife liked having a Harley Street husband, and giving little dinner parties in the suburbs with candlelight and sparkling wine.'

'Oh dear,' I said, giggling. 'Not quite your forte?'

'On the contrary, I look very good by candle-light. It was my fault as much as hers. She was beautiful, capable and absolutely bored me to death. I married her without really knowing her. Most people don't love human beings anyway. They just love an idealized picture in their heads.'

I looked at his face, softened now. I've never liked red hair, but Finn's was very dark and thick and grew beautifully close to his head. I've never liked freckles either, or broken noses, but he had extra-ordinary eyes, yellow-flecked, with thick black lashes, and his mouth, now it wasn't set in its usual hard line, was beautiful. The wind was blowing his trousers against his hard, muscular legs. He was in great shape, too. In spite of his size, he moved about the boat like a cat.

'Are you coming to Coco's party tonight?' I asked.

'I might,' he said. 'Depends what's up at the hospital.'

'Please come,' I said, then blushed. 'I mean, if you're not too busy.'

Chapter Eighteen

Rory was in the bath when I got back, wearing my bath cap but still managing to look absurdly handsome.

'Come in,' he said. 'I'm indecent. Where have you been?'

'Out and about,' I said. 'Can I have that bath after you?'

I went into the bedroom. I didn't want to tell him about Finn.

He followed me, dripping from the bath.

'Where's my white silk shirt?' he asked.

'Oh, er, I'm glad you asked that question.'

'Is this it?' he said, pulling a crumpled pink rag of a shirt out of the pillowcase of washing on the bed.

'Well, it could be,' I said.

'God,' said Rory. He went on pulling crumpled pink shirts out like a conjurer whipping out coloured handkerchiefs. 'How do you manage it?' he asked.

'I left one of my red silk scarves in the machine by mistake,' I said, miserably.

'Next time you want to do some dyeing, just count me out,' he said, and starting to get dressed, he put both feet into one leg of his underpants and fell over, which didn't improve his temper.

'How was Edinburgh?' I said, knowing that Marina had her singing lesson there once a fortnight.

He paused a second too long. 'I've been to Glasgow,' he said, evenly.

Rubbed raw with rancour, we arrived at the party. It was a dazzling affair, all the locals done up to the eyeballs in wool tweed. I was wearing about a quarter as much clothing as everyone else.

'Pretty as a picture,' said Buster, coming and squeezing me.

'Happy Birthday,' said Rory. 'I thought of buying you a book, Buster, but I knew you'd already got one.'

I heard someone laugh behind us. It was Marina, looking ravishing in a high-necked, amber wool dress with long sleeves. I'd forgotten about her being so beautiful. Since Christmas, she had become, in my tortured imagination, a sort of man-eating gorgon, with snakes writhing in her hair and corpses strewn about her feet. She smiled into Rory's eyes and went over to say hello to Coco.

Even the high-necked dress couldn't conceal two dark bruises under her chin.

'She's got love bites all over her neck,' I hissed at Rory out of the corner of my mouth.

'I suppose you recognize the teeth marks,' he hissed back.

'Well, they couldn't be Hamish's,' I said. 'He hasn't got any teeth left.'

'E-m-ilee,' said Rory quietly, 'you've got very bitchy since I married you.'

'You were bitchy before I married you!' I snapped.

'It must be catching.'

The party was a roaring success.

Everyone drank a great deal too much. I was sitting on the sofa with Rory several hours later, when Marina came up and sat down beside us.

'Hello darlings. I've decided to give up Hamish for Lent. Do you think Elizabeth's dress quite comes off?' she added, pointing at a fat blonde.

'It will do later in the evening, if I know Elizabeth,' said Rory.

Buster came up and filled up our drinks.

'Hello, Emily,' he said. 'You look a bit bleak. Not having words with Rory, I hope.'

'Rory and I don't have words any more, we just have silences,' I said, getting somewhat unsteadily to my feet.

'Come back,' said Rory. 'Buster wants to look down your dress.'

But I fled out of the room, falling over Buster's labrador who took it in extremely bad part. Why didn't Finn come? Every time the doorbell rang I hoped it was him. People were dancing in the dining-room now. I talked for hours to some dreary laird with a haw-haw voice and a come-heather look in his eye.

Hamish came up to us. He looked greyer and more haggard than ever, but his eyes had lost none of their goatish gleam.

'Emily,' he said, 'I haven't talked to you all evening. Come and dance.'

How could I refuse? On the dance floor, Rory and Marina were swaying very respectably, two feet apart. It was just the way they were looking at each other, like souls in torment.

'Just like lovebirds, aren't they?' said Hamish bitterly.

I looked at him startled.

'On second thoughts,' he said, 'it's time you and I had a little chat.'

He led me into a study off the hall, and shut the door. My heart was thumping unpleasantly.

'What do you want?' I said.

'Just to talk. Doesn't that little ménage upset you?'

'What ménage?' I said quickly.

'My lovely wife and your handsome husband. We've each been dealt a marked card, darling. Neither of them gives a damn about us.'

'I don't want to listen,' I said, going towards the door.

'But you must,' he said, catching my arm, his face suddenly alight with malevolence. 'It's quite a story. When Marina married me six months ago, I was foolish enough to think she cared for me. But, within weeks, I realized she only wanted me for my money.'

'If she was after money,' I said, 'why didn't she marry Rory? He's just as rich as you are.'

'Just as rich,' said Hamish. 'But Rory, if you remember, only inherited his money after he married you. That was one of the conditions of Rory's father, Hector's, will. Rory wouldn't get a bean until he was safely married.'

'Then why didn't he marry Marina?'

'That was another condition of the will. Hector made another condition that if he married Marina, he wouldn't get a penny. It would all go to charity. So he married you to get his hands on the cash.'

I felt myself go icy cold.

'But I don't understand,' I whispered. 'That doesn't sound like Rory at all. If he'd really wanted to marry Marina, he wouldn't have cared a damn about not inheriting the money. He could easily have got a job, or earned money from his painting, if he'd wanted to.'

'Oh, my poor child,' said Hamish mockingly. 'What a lot you've got to learn. Can't you under-stand that it's not possible for Rory ever to marry Marina, money or no money?'

'Why not?' I said.

'Because they're brother and sister.'

'What!' I gasped in horror. 'They can't be.'

'I'm afraid so. Hector, laird of the island, Lord Lieutenant, pillar of respectability on the surface, was an old ram on the side. Like claiming *droit de seigneur* and all that. He was very keen on Marina's mother for a long time. I'm afraid the result was Marina.'

I felt as though I was going to faint.

'Brother and sister,' I whispered again.

'Well, half-brother and -sister. Hardly a healthy union. Particularly as there's always been a strong strain of insanity in Hector's family. But it doesn't seem to deter them, does it?'

'How long have they known?' I muttered.

'Only about a year. There's always been a blood feud between the Balniels and the Macleans, as you know. So when Rory and Marina fell in love, they didn't exactly broadcast the fact, until one night Rory got drunk and had a row with Hector (they never really got on) and told him he was going to marry Marina. Hector nearly burst a gut. The next day he told Rory the truth, and that under no circumstances could he marry Marina. Rory went berserk with rage. The shock killed Hector. He died that night of a heart attack. But the will still stood.'

'My God,' I said, dully.

'So Marina married me in a fit of despair,' Hamish went on. 'And Rory went south and married you, which drove Marina mad with jealousy. And now, as you see, they're up to their old tricks.'

My brain was reeling. I felt as if I'd been kicked in the gut. Marina and Rory, brother and sister: Byron and Augusta Leigh, star-crossed lovers, a union so fatally seductive because it was impossible.

'Oh, poor Rory,' I breathed, 'now I understand. Oh, poor, poor Rory.'

'Poor you and me,' breathed Hamish in my ear.

He was standing very close to me, one hand fondling my wrist, his eyes fixed on my face in a greedy way. I could feel the warmth of his body, his hand stealing up my bare arm, his hot breath on my shoulder.

'You mustn't be shy of me, little Emily,' he said caressingly, slipping his arm round my waist. 'I think you're very pretty, even if Rory doesn't. Why don't we console one another?'

'No!' I screamed. 'No, no, no! Go away, you revolting old man. Don't touch me!'

I leapt to my feet, ran across the room, wrenched open the door and went slap into Finn Maclean.

'Hello,' he said. 'I've been looking for you.' Then he looked at me more closely. 'Hey, what's the matter?'

'Nothing, everything,' I sobbed, and shoving him violently aside, I fled past him.

I ran out into the garden. It had been snowing again, the drive was virginally white in the pale moonlight. All was deathly silent. The snow lay soft and tender on the lawn. Crying great, heaving sobs,

I ran to the edge of the cliffs. The sea stretched out, opaque, black and star-powdered. The lighthouse flashed like a blue gem, the rocks gleamed evilly two hundred feet below.

'Oh, Rory,' I sobbed. 'I can't go on, I can't go on.'

But as I took a step forward, my arm was caught in a vice-like grip.

'Don't be a bloody little fool,' said a voice. 'Nothing's that important.'

It was Finn.

'Let me go,' I sobbed. 'I want to die.'

He held on to my arm and finally I collapsed against him.

'Oh, Finn,' I sobbed. 'What am I going to do?'

He held me for a minute, then, putting an arm round my shoulders, he half carried me across the snow to the stables where Buster kept his horses.

I collapsed on to a pile of hay, still sobbing bitterly. Finn let me cry; he just sat there stroking my shoulders. Finally I gulped, 'It's not true, is it, Marina and Rory both being Hector's children?'

Finn paused, his hand tightening on my shoulder, then he said, 'It is, I'm afraid.'

'Oh, God,' I said. 'Why didn't anyone tell me?'

'No-one knew except me and Rory and Marina. Marina must have told Hamish. Even Coco doesn't know about it.'

'How long have you known?' I said dully.

'As long as I can remember. I got back from school early one afternoon. I heard laughter coming from the bedroom and went in and found my mother in bed with Hector. My father was away at the time. I ran and hid in the woods. My father came home that night and sent out a search party. When they found me, my father thrashed me for worrying my mother. I never told him the truth. I suppose kids have a sort of honour even at that age. But I never forgave Hector, and he never forgave me for discovering what an old fraud he was.'

'So you always knew Rory and Marina were brother and sister?'

He nodded. 'About a year ago, I came back from London for a weekend and discovered, to my horror, they'd fallen in love and were thinking of getting married. I tried to stop Marina, but she'd got the bit between her teeth by then, so I went to Hector and told him he'd got to tell Rory the truth.'

'Not a very pretty story, is it?' I said.

'That's why I've been behaving like a policeman, trying to keep them apart,' said Finn. 'With insanity on both sides and a blood tie between them, it would be absolutely fatal if Rory got Marina pregnant.'

I sat numbly, trying to take it all in. Finn was holding me in his arms now, stroking my hair, soothing me like a child. I felt the hardness of his body, the gentleness of his hands. It was so long since I'd been in a man's arms. I've always said I have no sense of timing.

His mouth was so near to mine. Almost instinctively, I put my face up and kissed him. The next moment he was kissing me back.

'Heavens,' I said, wriggling away, absolutely appalled. 'I'm terribly sorry.'

'Don't be,' he said softly. 'It's one of the nicest surprises I've ever had,' and he kissed me again. This time it was a kiss that meant business. I tried to be frigid and unyielding, but could feel the warm waves of lust coasting all over me. I felt my body go weak. I was torn between desire and utter exhaustion.

'Strange things happen in stables,' I muttered weakly. 'One moment I'm a midwife, next moment I'm bowling towards adultery. Talk about My Tart Is In The Highlands.'

Finn smiled, got up and pulled me to my feet.

'Come on, I'm taking you home.'

'Please don't,' I said.

'Listen,' he said. 'I never meant this to happen when I brought you in here. I want you very much, but I think now is neither the time nor the place. You're slightly drunk and you're suffering from severe shock. I'm not going to let you do anything you might regret in the morning.'

He drove me home. Outside the house he burrowed in his bag and produced a couple of sleeping pills.

'Take them tonight, immediately you get in, and come and see me at the surgery tomorrow at eleven. Then we can talk things over.'

When I got in I hardly had the strength to undress. I fell, rather than got, into bed, pulled the sheets like a curtain over my head and dropped into a deep sleep.

Chapter Nineteen

I woke up next morning feeling ghastly, went straight to the loo and was violently sick. I had a blinding headache, took four Alka-Seltzers and was sick again. Rory was still fast asleep.

I tiptoed around the bedroom getting my clothes on. I only just managed to make it to Finn's surgery.

There was only one woman in there when I arrived. Finn came out. He looked tired, but he smiled at me reassuringly.

'I'll just see Mrs Cameron first,' he said. 'She won't take long.'

I gazed unseeingly at magazines and wondered why I was feeling quite so awful. Finn's receptionist eyed me with interest.

Mrs Balniel looking like a road accident, she must have been thinking.

Mrs Cameron came out, thanking Finn effusively, and I went into his surgery.

It was large, and rather untidy, and amazingly comforting. Finn shut the door and leant against it. Then he came across the room and kissed me. It was a different kiss from last night. That was alcohol and pent-up emotion. This was slow, measured, tender, and left me just as weak with lust.

'Aren't we doing fearful things to the Hippocratic Oath?' I said, flopping on to a chair.

'I couldn't give a damn. You aren't my patient yet, though you ought to be, you look terrible!'

'Thanks,' I said.

'And infinitely desirable. Nothing a few weeks away from Rory wouldn't cure.'

'I was as sick as a dog all morning,' I said. 'Nerves and booze, I suppose.'

'I'll tell Miss Bates to shove off, then I'll give you a going over.'

'You'd better wipe that lipstick off first,' I said.

Finn laughed.

He wasn't laughing half an hour later.

'You're pregnant,' he said.

I was stunned by the news. 'But I can't be pregnant!' I gasped. 'Rory hasn't laid a finger on me for months.' Then I remembered. 'Oh, God,' I said.

'What's the matter?' asked Finn.

'After that row on Christmas Eve when you knocked Rory over, he was so mad with rage, he sort of raped me.'

'That must have been it,' said Finn.

My brain was whirling. Me – pregnant with Rory's child! What sort of chance would a baby have with Rory not loving me, and me fancying Finn absolutely rotten all of a sudden? I had a nightmare vision of Rory and me shouting at each other across the baby's cot, of the baby crying all day, and Rory going spare because he couldn't work.

'Oh, heavens,' I said shakily.

Finn went to a cupboard in the corner of the room and got out a bottle of brandy and two glasses. 'We'd better have a drink,' he said.

As I watched him fill the glasses, I was filled with a ridiculous mawkish sadness. I'll never be able to memorize every freckle on his face now, I thought, or see the grey hairs gradually take the fire out of that red mane.

He put a glass beside me, then took hold of my frozen hands. His were warm and strong and comforting; I felt an irresistible urge to collapse in tears on his shoulder.

'It's a hell of a mess,' he said gently, 'but it doesn't matter, we'll sort something out.'

'Can we?' I asked dolefully.

'Look,' he went on. 'You and Rory are washed up. Anyone can see that. Do you want to keep the baby?'

I thought for a minute. 'Yes I do. Very much.'

'That means you'll stay with Rory?'

'What else can I do?' I said bitterly. 'I'm signed up for this gig and I've got to play.'

'You can move in with me.'

The room reeled. For a moment all I could think of was the blissful sanctity of Finn taking care of me.

'Oh, Finn,' I said, the tears welling up in my eyes, 'I'd drive you round the twist.'

'I wouldn't think so. We can always try.'

'But what about the baby?'

He shrugged his shoulders.

'It's Rory's,' I said, taking a slug of my brandy and nearly choking. 'You'd hate that, you'd keep seeing all the things you hate about Rory in its character. And your reputation on the island would be absolutely ruined – your worst enemy's wife shacking up with you, and pregnant to boot.'

'*My* reputation can take it,' said Finn.

'Is it because you want to score off Rory by taking me away from him?' I blurted out.

It was a terrible thing to say. Rory would have certainly hit me for it, but Finn merely looked at me consideringly.

'I don't know,' he said. 'I thought about that for a long time last night, after I'd dropped you off. Of course there's an element of truth. I don't have any compunction about taking you away from Rory. I know he's made you miserable and unhappy. But even if you were married to my best friend, I don't think it would make any difference. I'd still want you. It's one of the unattractive things about loving someone – one just suspends all moral values.' Then his face softened. 'But there are an awful lot of attractive things about it. Come here.'

'No,' I said desperately. 'Please, no.'

He held out his hands. 'Why not? I want you.'

'It's very noble of you to make the offer, but I couldn't.'

'Noble! What the hell are you talking about?'

'I know why you're asking me. It's from motives of altruism. Marina's your sister and you feel guilty about the way she and Rory have fouled up my life.'

Finn drained his glass. 'Emily, will you please stop talking nonsense! I'm the least altruistic person alive. Apart from being a doctor, I never do anything to please anyone except myself.'

'You took me sailing yesterday . . .'

'Look,' said Finn, 'I took you sailing yesterday because I thought you needed a break. Now I realize I've wanted you since the first moment I saw you – pulling up my roses with your teeth – in a black see-through nightie.'

'Oh,' I felt myself blushing furiously. 'How kind of you to put it like that.'

'And you don't believe a word of it?'

'No, you'd never have asked me to move in with you if I hadn't been pregnant.' I searched feverishly for a tissue and mopped my eyes.

'Of course I wouldn't,' said Finn. 'I'd have taken it more slowly.'

'There's absolutely no point in shacking up with someone one hardly knows, who one's not in love with,' I said shakily. That stopped him.

'I suppose not,' he said grimly.

I gave my eyes a final wipe.

'I'm sorry. I don't mean to keep crying – it's the

shock of the baby, and finding out about Rory and Marina last night. And, besides, I'd be hopeless for you – I mean long-term. I don't have the right face for greeting patients, and I'd forget to pass on messages about cardiacs and things.'

'We can still go on seeing each other.'

'No,' I said. 'When you're pregnant you can't go around carrying on with other people. I mean it turns you into a sort of nun, having a baby.'

Finn laughed, but bitterly. 'You know, do you? From your quarter of an hour's experience. You'll still have to come in for check-ups. If you don't want to see me, I suppose Jackie Barrett can look after you.'

'Who's she?'

'My new intern.'

Oh, God, I minded about her. I minded like hell. I fought back the tears. I didn't dare kiss Finn, or I might have broken down.

'Goodbye and thank you,' I said.

Finn looked suddenly tired and defeated. 'All right, go back to Rory if you want to, but remember I'm here. You've only to pick up a telephone and I'll come and take you away.'

Chapter Twenty

Which wasn't a very good basis for trying to rebuild
a marriage. When I got home, I was all screwed up
to tell Rory about the baby, but he was so immersed
in slapping blue paint on a huge canvas, absolutely
lost to the world, that I funked it and so, having not
told him, I found it more and more difficult.

In fact, he was so obsessed with work for the next
few weeks, he hardly noticed me at all.

I thought endlessly about the baby. No more
staying in the cinema to see the film once again – got
to get home to the baby-sitter. No more running
away to sea. I thought of dirty nappies and sleepless
nights, and maternity bras, and getting bigger and
heavier, and less attractive to Rory.

But somehow, I felt excited too. Growing inside
was something that, when it arrived, would really
need me. Something I could love totally and
unashamedly, as I wanted to love Rory, as circumstances had stopped me loving Finn.

I kept wanting to tell Rory. I bought a bottle of
champagne, and day after day took it out of its

hiding place at the back of a drawer, then funked it and put it away.

I made a concerted attempt to win Rory over sexually, but it had been 'God, I'm tired', for days now. As soon as I got into bed, he'd switch off his light, turn his back on me, and pretend to be asleep.

And I'd lie beside him, tears sliding into my hair, listening to the sea washing on the rocks below and thinking of Finn, who was probably still working, going out to deliver a baby or soothing a restless patient. His harsh, beautifully ugly face would swim before my eyes, and I would wonder how much longer I could hold out.

I went to every party on the island too, in the hope that I might see him, but he never turned up. Which meant I drank too much and was even sicker the morning after.

I did see Miss Barrett, the new intern, though. I couldn't resist having a gawp. I went in for a check-up and had a great shock. She was naturally blonde, and slim – one of those women who look marvellous without make-up – deep, subtle, competent, able to keep her mouth shut. The antithesis of me.

Did I imagine, too, an added warmth in her voice when she talked about Finn? Dr Maclean likes things done this way. Dr Maclean doesn't approve of pregnant women putting on too much weight. Dr Maclean recommends these vitamin pills.

'And Dr Maclean recommends me,' I wanted to

shout at her. 'He's mine, and trespassers will be very much prosecuted.'

The weeks passed. Slowly I sank into despair. I could hardly bring myself to get up in the morning and get dressed. One Sunday morning, however, when I was trying to keep down some toast and marmalade, I suddenly caught Rory looking at me.

'You look awful,' he said. 'What are you trying to turn yourself into?'

Then followed a ten-minute invective about my general attitude towards him and everyone else on the island. I was lazy, childish, stubborn, stupid and unco-operative. Why didn't I do something instead of slopping around all day?

'What do you think I should be doing? Going to evening classes, exchanging meaningful glances over the basket-work and all that?' I said.

'Maybe; you could go out more, see people. Buster offered you his horses anytime you wanted to ride. Anything but this plastic tomb you've sealed yourself into.'

'Have you finished?' I whispered.

'Yes, for the time being. I'm sorry I came on so strong. I didn't mean to be quite so vicious, but I'm fed up with sharing a house with a zombie.'

I got up without looking at him and dragged myself upstairs. He was right. One look at myself in the mirror sent me yelping to the bathroom to wash my hair.

Then I rang Buster and asked if I could come and

ride with him that afternoon. Rory was absurdly pleased and even rubbed my hair dry for me.

'Stay over at the castle when you've finished,' he said. 'I'll come over and take you all out to dinner.'

For the first time in months he kissed me.

Buster and I rode up the lower slopes through beech trees between mossy rocks. Walter Scott ran about, snorting and chasing rabbits. Finally we reached the top.

'Hospital's finished now,' said Buster, pointing his whip at the new building on the right. 'Finn's got it up jolly fast. Have you been inside?'

I shook my head.

Buster's voice – the usual mixture of sex, gin and a dash of bitters – flowed on. 'Have you seen Finn's new popsy?'

I stiffened. 'Popsy?'

'Dr Barrett,' went on Buster. 'She's an absolute smasher. Took my lumbago to see her last week – can hardly keep my hands off her.'

'Are she and Finn having a walk-out?' I asked.

'Why do you think he brought her up here?' said Buster, as though it were a matter of course. 'Finn isn't daft.'

Black gloom overwhelmed me as I rode back down the hill. Finn in love with someone else. That left Rory and me, didn't it?

'I think I'll go straight home now,' I said.

'Isn't Rory taking us out to dinner?' asked Buster.

'He is,' I said, 'but there's something I want to tell him first. And I want to change too.'

We stabled the horses, and as I drove back home I decided now was the time to tell Rory about the baby.

'We'll have to face the music together, mate,' I said to the child inside me. 'Maybe he'll surprise us and be delighted after all.'

I went into the house and tiptoed upstairs to get the champagne. The bedroom door was open.

And I caught them red-handed.

Chapter Twenty-one

Marina and Rory in bed. For a second all I could think was how beautiful they looked on my dark blue sheets – her glorious mass of red hair cascading all over the pillows. Just like a Hollywood film. Two people too beautiful for real life.

Then I screamed and they looked round. Marina recovered from the shock first.

'I'm sorry, Emily,' she said. 'But you had to know sometime.'

'Oh, I've known,' I said. 'I've known for ages and I've known too about your being brother and sister.'

That rocked them.

'I mean, it's nice your keeping it in the family,' I went on, 'but that sort of thing is rather frowned on in the prayer book and by the law, I should think.'

I ran out of the room, locked myself in the loo and started to cry. After a few minutes someone came and rattled on the door.

'Go away!' I screamed. 'Use the other loo. This one's engaged.'

'Emily, it's me. Marina's gone. For God's sake come out. I want to help you.'

'Help me?' I felt my tears escalating into hysterical laughter. 'Help me? What can you do to help me?'

'Let me in, or I'll break the door down.'

'No!' I screamed. 'No! No!' There was a silence, and then an explosion.

I screamed again. The door was swinging and Rory was standing in the doorway, a smoking gun in his hand. He'd shot the lock out.

'Now, come out!' he said, grabbing my arm and dragging me into the bedroom. Walter Scott sat whimpering in the corner.

'I know why you married me,' I hissed. 'Just to release the cash from Hector's will, to give you a front of respectability so you could carry on with Marina, your dear little sister.'

Rory was trembling. 'Who told you all this?' he said.

'Hamish did,' I said.

'He's a swine,' said Rory.

'He's unhappy,' I said. 'He didn't want anyone to be left out. He certainly hasn't behaved any worse than you.'

'When you're desperate, you suspend any kind of morality,' Rory said, echoing Finn's words of two months before.

Then he told me, quietly and without any emotion, that when he'd first met me, he'd been very attracted to me, had thought I was so gentle, loving and understanding, that we might even make a go of it. He said he had intended, had tried desperately hard, to break it off with Marina, but had failed to do so. And there was nothing he could plead by way of excuse or justification. Volcanoes of invective and abuse kept boiling up inside me, and sinking down again. It was his detachment that paralysed my powers of speech. But for the cold, fixed shadows in his eyes, and his deathly pallor, he seemed his normal self.

'Marina and I do realize we're social pariahs, in the wilderness for good and all. She's upset, of course, because she can't have my children.'

'She's upset,' I breathed. 'Oh, boy, do I feel sympathy for her. I suppose it's more exciting, doing it here in our bed. It's much more exotic than turning on ten miles away where I couldn't possibly catch you.'

He looked at me. Did I imagine there was a flicker of despair in his eyes.

Then he said the fatal words.

'I'm sorry, Em.'

'Get out,' I hissed. 'Get out! Get out.'

He stood irresolute for a minute.

'I don't want to spend another minute under the same roof as you,' I said.

I suppose that was the cue he wanted. Within two minutes he'd thrown his things into a suitcase and Walter and he were gone.

Whimpering with terror, I rushed to the telephone.

I recognized Jackie Barrett's voice immediately. There was music in the background.

'Can I speak to Dr Maclean?' I said.

'Just a minute.' How cool and off-hand she sounded. 'Is it urgent? He's very tied up at the moment.'

'Yes it is. Very urgent.'

'Who's that speaking?'

'It's personal.'

'Finn, darling,' she said, and I could just imagine her turning up her palms in a gesture of helplessness. 'I'm afraid it's for you.'

I slammed down the receiver.

Rory gone. Finn obviously taken care of by Dr Barrett. That left the baby and me.

'You're the only thing I've got now,' I said numbly.

It wouldn't take me long to pack my suitcase, either. If I hurried I could catch the seven o'clock ferry.

I rang for a taxi.

When the doorbell rang I grabbed Rory's dark glasses to hide my swollen eyes, gathered up my two suitcases and walked to the top of the stairs. I suppose I must have missed the top step. The next moment I was falling. The pain was something I'd never known or could ever have imagined. The rest was blackness.

Chapter Twenty-two

Through a haze of pain, I kept dreaming of Marina and Rory in bed together, writhing like snakes on those navy-blue sheets.

Then I heard a familiar voice say, 'The doses have been exceptionally strong, but her reflexes are much better.'

A woman's voice said, 'It's unlikely we'll get a peep out of her for twenty-four hours.'

Painfully, battling with nausea, I opened my eyes and there, miraculously, was Finn standing at the end of the bed talking to a nurse.

The image of Rory and Marina floated back in front of me, and I screamed.

Finn moved like lightning.

'Darling Emily, it's me.'

I went on screaming and yelling incoherently. He had his arms round me. 'I'll deal with her,' he said. The nurse melted away.

I sat rigid. 'I remember everything that happened,' I said.

'It's Finn, Emily darling.'

161

I stopped screaming and collapsed against him. 'Oh, Finn! Help me!'

'You've had a bad dream.'

'I remember everything.' My lips began to tremble. 'You promise not to do anything to find Rory? Not anything!'

'Don't worry,' he reassured me.

He persuaded me to lie back on the pillows, but kept a firm grip on my hand.

'Don't go away,' I whispered.

'I'm staying right here.'

'I thought you didn't want me any more, and then I found Rory and Marina . . .'

'Steady, darling, don't think about it. You're going to get better.'

'But I saw them in bed together! I saw them!'

The edge of the cliff began to crumble. I started to scream and lash about. The nurse came back with a hypodermic syringe. I tried to struggle, but Finn held me still. Whatever it was they gave me worked instantly.

Next time I surfaced, I was calmer. I was in an ugly, fawn but sunny room. A fat nurse was arranging some daffodils in a blue vase. There were flowers everywhere. 'Is this a funeral parlour?' I asked.

She rushed over and started fumbling with my pulse.

'Where am I?'

'In hospital.'

'Good old hospital. With hot and cold housemen in every bedroom.'

'I'll get Dr Maclean,' she said, and belted off. I heard mutterings in the passage about 'still being delirious'. Finn walked into the room.

'Jump in, Doctor,' I said, 'we'll be delirious together.'

'It sounds as though she's recovered,' Finn said to the nurse.

He was one of those rewarding men who can betray emotion in public. His yellow eyes were filled with tears as he looked down at me.

'Hello, baby.'

'Hello,' I said.

'Don't try to talk.'

'I missed you,' I said, 'I missed you horribly.'

He smiled. 'I suppose you must have. You talked enough in your sleep.' He looked absolutely grey with tiredness. The dope they'd given me had removed every vestige of my self-control. 'I do love you,' I said. 'You've got such a lovely face.'

They kept me under gradually reduced sedation for the first forty-eight hours, bringing me back to earth slowly. I can't remember when the baby drifted back into my consciousness, but I remember suddenly saying to Finn in panic, 'The baby? It's all right, isn't it?'

He took my hand. 'I'm afraid you lost it. We tried to save it, darling, you must believe that.'

I felt gripped by a piercing sadness. Then I said, 'Where's Rory?'

'He's fine.'

I said: 'Where's Rory? Tell me the truth, Finn.'

The yellow eyes flickered for a moment. 'He hasn't come back. He must be on the mainland somewhere.'

'With Marina?'

He nodded. 'I presume so. She disappeared the night you fell down the stairs. Neither of them has been seen since.'

Chapter Twenty-three

I lay in my hospital bed for I don't know how many days, dully watching the beauty of the Highland spring. Among this building of nests and mating of birds and animals, I felt alien and outcast. I ached for the baby I had lost. A brisk, bossy nurse looked after me, Nurse McKellen. She had come-to-bedpan eyes, and tried to fill me up with pills and pretty revolting food.

'Couldn't I have a nurse with a sense of humour?' I asked Finn.

'Not on the Health Service,' he said.

I longed inordinately for his visits. He used to pop in during the mornings or late in the evenings after visiting hours and just sit holding my hand and telling me about his day, or letting me rave on about Rory and the baby, if I felt like it.

Once, when Jackie Barrett came in, he didn't even let go of my hand.

'She's getting better,' he told her.

'Good,' she said crisply. 'You gave us all a fright,' she added to me.

I thought I detected a few chips of ice in her blue eyes.

'I thought you were having an *affaire* with her,' I said after she'd gone.

Finn looked surprised.

'She answered the telephone the night I rang, and sounded awfully proprietorial.'

'She had no need to,' said Finn. 'We were only watching some medical programme on television.'

After that I felt much happier. I slept a lot. Finn still wouldn't allow me any visitors and I didn't want any. But at the back of my mind was a great deal of dread and expectation. I didn't have to wait long.

Two days later I was lying in bed half asleep.

Suddenly there was a commotion outside and a familiar voice saying impatiently, 'Where is she?'

Immediately I was awake and drenched with sweat, my pulses pounding.

'Don't be so bloody stupid,' continued the voice. 'I'm her husband!'

Then Nurse McKellen's voice, anxious and flustered. 'I'm sorry, Dr Maclean's orders are that she has no visitors.'

'Then I'll go through the wards waking every patient till I find her.'

'You dinna understand, sir, Mrs Balniel's been verra ill. She had severe concussion and internal haemorrhage as well, and she's been very depressed since she regained consciousness, learning about losing the baby, poor wee lassie.'

'The what?' Rory's voice was like the crack of a whip. 'What did you say?'

'Since she lost the bairn. You must have been disappointed too, sir?'

Then Rory's voice hissing through his teeth. 'Where is she, damn you?'

And Nurse McKellen's high-pitched shriek. 'Don't you lay your hands on me, young man! All right, Mrs Balniel's in there, but I'll no answer for Dr Maclean when he comes back.'

I heard a quick step outside. A moment later the door was flung open and in strode Rory. 'So there you are.'

'Hello, Rory,' I croaked.

He was beside the bed, black eyes blazing, his face deathly pale against the black fur of his coat.

'What's this about a baby?' he demanded. 'Is it true?'

I nodded.

'How long had you known?'

'About two months.'

'Why the hell didn't you tell me?'

'I tried to,' I said miserably. 'I wanted to so badly. I just didn't feel up to it.'

'And you threw me out without even letting me know of its existence!'

'I didn't think you'd be interested.'

'Not interested in my own child?'

'Mr Balniel.' It was Nurse McKellen again, her starched bosom heaving. 'We mustn't disturb Mrs Balniel.'

Rory didn't turn his head.

'Get out, you fat bitch,' he said.

Then, when she didn't he turned on her. One look at the murderous expression on his face and she scarpered.

'How did it happen?' he asked.

'I was wearing your dark glasses. I must have missed the top step of the stairs and conked out when I hit the bottom.'

'I suppose you don't remember anything about it?' he said.

'Not much,' I said slowly, 'but I remember very vividly what happened before.'

Rory side-stepped the issue. 'Why the hell couldn't you have told me about the baby before?' he said. 'It was criminally irresponsible of you, I hope you realize that?'

'I knew you were in love with Marina,' I said feebly. 'If I'd told you about the baby you'd have thought I was trying to trap you.'

'That's the most fatuous remark I've ever heard,' snapped Rory. 'I suppose it *was* my child?'

I burst into tears. At that moment Finn walked in. He was livid. You could feel the hatred sizzling between the two men like summer lightning.

'What's going on?' Finn said to Nurse McKellen.

'Make him go away,' I sobbed.

'Leave her alone,' thundered Finn. 'Get out of here. Do you want her to have a complete relapse?'

'She's my wife,' said Rory, 'I'm entitled to stay with her.'

'Not if you're going to make her ill. Look at her.'

Finn sat down on the bed and put his arms round me. 'There lovie, it's all right.'

'I can't take any more,' I sobbed into Finn's shoulder. 'Please make him go away.'

Finn looked up. Rory was ashen, his fists clenched.

'Now are you going to get out?' said Finn.

Rory walked out, slamming the door behind him.

Chapter Twenty-four

Next day Finn flew round the island to visit his patients, and Rory rolled up at visiting time. He looked tired, sulky, unshaven, but still illogically handsome.

Oh, please, don't let me fall under his spell again.

He brought with him a huge bunch of lilies-of-the-valley, two tins of *pâté de foie gras*, a pornographic novel and a bottle of Lucozade.

'The meat paste is from my mother,' he said. 'Buster sent the piece of porn. He said he enjoyed it, which is no great recommendation. They all send love.'

Then he handed me the Lucozade bottle.

'This should get you through the long evenings. It's whisky and water actually, but if you keep the top on I defy even Dr Maclean to tell the difference.'

I giggled. 'How did you get in here?' I said. 'I should have thought Finn would have put bloodhounds on the gates.'

'I batted my eyelashes at a rather formidable

170

blonde called Dr Barrett. She said I could see you for a quarter of an hour.'

'That figures,' I said.

'How are you?' I asked.

'I'm fine,' said Rory.

'Who's looking after you?' I said, then blushed furiously. 'I mean . . . I didn't mean to pry.'

'No-one's looking after me,' he said.

I was dying to ask where Marina was, but suddenly I felt exhausted, like a hostess at the end of a party when no-one's enjoyed themselves.

'You don't have to stay,' I said. 'It's awfully boring visiting people in hospital.'

'Sick of me already, are you?'

I looked up and he was staring at me, as if for the first time. He went on staring until I dropped my eyes in embarrassment.

He got up to go. 'I'll come back tomorrow,' he said. 'I'm sorry about the baby.'

Then he did the strangest thing. He leant forward and did up the four undone buttons of my nightie.

'I don't want Finn looking at your tits,' he said.

He turned up every day after that. Neither of us mentioned Marina. I was surprised how nice he could be – not mocking, not bored, but I found his visits a terrible strain. If Finn knew about them, he didn't say anything.

One day, a week later, a heavily pregnant girl was rushed into the room next door to have her baby. She was very young and frightened, and her husband looked even younger and more scared. But their tenderness for one another made me once again realize what I had lost.

When Finn came in later in his overcoat, just off on his rounds, he found me in tears.

He understood at once. 'Is it the girl next door?' he asked.

I nodded miserably. 'It's just triggered off memories,' I said.

'Don't be unhappy,' he said, putting his arms around me. 'There's years ahead for you to have babies.'

The door opened. I jumped and looked around. Rory stood in the doorway looking distinctly menacing. Going absolutely scarlet, I leapt away from Finn; then thought, why the hell should I after the way Rory's treated me?

'I thought you weren't coming until later,' I stammered.

'So I notice,' he snapped. 'Shall I leave you to it?'

'Don't be stupid,' I said. 'Finn's just off on his rounds.'

'I'm quite happy to stay here if you think you'll need protection,' Finn said.

Rory set his teeth and strolled in the middle of the room. A muscle was pounding in his cheek.

Before he could speak, I quickly said, 'I'm able to take care of myself, thanks.'

Rory glared furiously at Finn until he was out of the room. 'If you don't want me to smash the hell out of him, you'd better not start necking with him any more. OK?'

'Quite OK,' I said. 'But quite honestly, you're being fatuous. Only jealousy could merit such rage, and as you self-confessedly don't love me, why the hell should you be jealous?'

'I believe in protecting my own property,' said Rory.

'Anyway, he wasn't necking with me,' I said. 'He was comforting me. I was miserable about losing the baby.'

Rory came towards me, holding out his arms. 'It's me who ought to comfort you,' he said gently.

I shrank away from him, terrified. I started to cry.

'Oh, for Christ's sake,' he snapped.

'I'm not up to rows,' I bleated.

He prowled up and down the room. 'What a horrible place this is,' he said. 'It's time you came home.'

'I can't!' I yelped. 'I've been very ill. Finn says I'm not strong enough to go home yet!'

Chapter Twenty-five

Later that evening I tried to read Buster's pornographic novel while the little girl had her baby next door. I held my ears to blot out her screams, and the voice of her husband trying to reassure her. Finally, I heard the lusty yelling of the new-born baby.

Later, going out to the loo, I saw the husband outside the room, tears pouring down his face.

'Is she all right?' I asked.

He nodded. 'She's wonderful, and the baby's fine. A wee boy. We're going to call him Finn after Dr Maclean.'

'How would you like some whisky?' I said.

'I wouldna say no to a drop.'

I took him back to my room and got out the Lucozade bottle. An hour later we were sitting on my bed as tight as two ticks, laughing immoderately over passages in Buster's novel. It was Nurse McKellen who discovered us. She was absolutely appalled.

I escaped to the loo, giggling feebly. I felt very peculiar. 'At least I've got some colour in my cheeks,' I said, looking at my flushed, wild-eyed face in the mirror.

Outside, I found Finn. I looked down the passage. There was no-one there.

'Hello, darling,' I whispered.

'What have you been up to?' he said. 'Nurse McKellen's spreading terrifying tales of drunken orgies.'

I giggled and collapsed against him.

'You have been drinking,' he said.

'On the emptiest stomach in the Western Isles,' I said, 'and it's gone right down to my toes. I've been celebrating the birth of little Finn the second, and reading porn. So I feel fantastically sexy.'

Finn tried to look disapproving, and then laughed. I wound my arms round his neck and kissed him. After a minute's hesitation, he kissed me back, long and hard, until the blood was drumming in my head and I thought I was going to faint.

'Wow, do I feel sexy,' I murmured.

'How the hell do you think I feel?' he said.

A telephone shrilled in the next room.

'I'd better answer that,' he said. 'I'll deal with you later.'

'I've got you under my sk-in, I've got you de-heep in the heart of me,' I sang as I swayed down the passage, slap into Rory standing in the shadows. He must have seen everything.

'Oh, God,' I said, going briskly into reverse. He caught my arm and held on tightly.

'You bloody phoney,' he hissed. 'You bloody little phoney. All that *Dame aux Camelias* act. Not feeling well enough to get out of bed, you said. Depends on whose bed, doesn't it? Doctor Maclean won't let you leave. I bet he won't. You're having a ball together, aren't you – *aren't you*!' he yelled.

I looked around for a convenient second-floor window to jump out of.

'You don't understand,' I muttered.

'Oh, I do, baby, I understand only too well.'

The whole thing was getting too much for me. With a sigh I forced myself to look at him. I'd never seen him so cold with rage.

'You're coming home tonight, before you get up to any more tricks,' he said.

That moment Finn came out of the side door. I thought they'd have a right old set-to, but I was wrong. Finn had other things on his mind now.

'A petrol ship's blown up outside the harbour,' he said. 'They're bringing the survivors back in the life-boats. Most of them are likely to have second- or third-degree burns.'

'So you'll be needing all the beds you can get,' said Rory.

'Yes, we will,' said Dr Barrett, coming down the hall.

'I'll take Emily home then,' said Rory.

'That's an excellent idea,' said Dr Barrett warmly – the scheming cow.

Finn looked as though he was about to protest,

then thought better of it. 'If you can take her to the castle,' he said, 'where there's someone to look after her. See that she rests as much as possible.'

'Of course,' said Rory. 'Do you need any help?'

'I'll ring you if we do, but most of the poor bastards will have had it.'

'The ambulance is leaving, Finn,' said Jackie Barrett, going towards the stairs.

'Just coming,' said Finn. He looked at me as though he wanted to say something, but I could feel him sliding away, both mentally and physically.

'I'll ring tomorrow and see how you're getting on,' he said. Then he was gone.

I felt overwhelmed with desolation and fear.

'And now, Emily dear,' said Rory softly, 'I think it's time you came home.'

We didn't speak on the way back from the hospital, but as the castle loomed into view, Rory shot straight past it.

'Finn said you were to take me to the castle,' I bleated.

'You're coming home,' snapped Rory, 'where I can keep an eye on you.'

'You can't force me to stay with you.'

'I can – even if I have to strap you to the bed.'

'Go directly to jail,' I chanted. 'Do not pass go, do not collect £200.'

I steeled myself for chaos when we got home. But the house looked marvellous. Someone had obviously been having a massive blitz. Rory steered me into the studio. The canvases had all been stacked neatly into one corner, a huge log fire blazed, and the smell of wood smoke mingled exotically with the scent of a big bowl of blue hyacinths on the window-sill.

'Anyone would think you were expecting company,' I said.

'I was,' said Rory grimly. 'You. I came to the hospital to collect you.'

'Oh, very masterful,' I said, collapsing on to the divan in the corner.

Rory poured himself a good mahogany-coloured whisky.

'I'd like one, too,' I said.

'You've had enough,' he said.

He leaned against the mantelpiece, a long stick he had been about to throw into the fire in his hands. The expression on his face scared me – he was quite capable of beating me up.

'Now,' he said, 'just how long have you been having an affair with Maclean?'

'I haven't,' I said.

'Don't lie to me,' he thundered.

'Affairs begin below the waist,' I protested. 'All Finn has done is kiss me – three times, to be exact.'

'You counted them?'

'Yes I did! Because they mattered.'

'And where did all this restraint take place?'

'Finn looked after me the night I found out you and Marina were brother and sister. But the next day, as soon as I discovered I was pregnant, we stopped seeing each other. Tonight I'd been at the whisky and Buster's porny novel, so when I met Finn in the passage, I suddenly fancied him rotten.'

There was a crack – Rory had snapped the lath in his hands. He was silent for a minute, his face strangely dead, then he threw the broken sticks on the fire. 'You're nothing better than a tart,' he said.

'I don't want to be better than a tart,' I said. 'Men seem to rather like them.'

'Well it's got to stop,' said Rory.

'You have the teremity . . .' I said.

'Temerity,' interrupted Rory.

'I'll say teremity if I like. You have the terem . . . or whatever it's called . . . to carry on with Marina behind my back, and then kick up a dog-in-the-manger rumpus, just because I seek a little consolation from Finn. You're only livid because you hate Finn, not because you care a scrap for me.'

'Shut up,' said Rory. 'You're drunk – you'd better go up to bed.'

'No!' I shrieked. 'I can't do it.'

'Do what?'

'Sleep in that bed. Not after seeing you and Marina . . . I get nightmares night after night . . . I couldn't sleep there, I couldn't!' My voice was rising hysterically.

Rory caught my arm. 'Stop it, Em! You're behaving like a child.'

'Let me go!' I screamed. 'I hate you. I hate you!'

After that I said every terrible thing I could think of, and then started hysterically beating my fists against his chest. Finally, he was reduced to slapping me across the face, and I collapsed, sobbing, on the divan.

Chapter Twenty-six

I awoke next morning with an awful head. I lay for a moment with my eyes closed. Slowly, painfully, I pieced together the happenings of the night before. I looked around me, wincing. I was in the studio.

Then, suddenly, I remembered Rory had hit me. 'The louse,' I muttered, getting unsteadily to my feet. In the mirror above the fire, I examined my face. Not a bruise in sight – how infuriating. My eyes lit on Rory's oil paints on a nearby table. Why shouldn't I paint in a black eye myself?

Soon I was busy slapping on blue and crimson paint – now a touch of yellow. Rory wasn't the only artist round here. Within five minutes I looked exactly like Henry Cooper after a few brisk rounds with Cassius Clay. Hearing a step outside, I hurriedly jumped into bed.

Rory came in, carrying a glass of orange juice.

'Awake, are you?' he said. 'How are you feeling?'

'Not very good,' I quavered.

'Don't deserve to, after all that liquor you shipped.'

Then he caught sight of the bruise.

'Heavens! Where did that come from?'

'I think you must have hit me,' I said in a martyred voice. 'I don't remember much about it – it must have been quite a blow. But I can't really believe you would have thumped me on my first night home – me being so weak and all. Perhaps I bumped into a door.'

Rory looked as discomfited as I've ever seen him.

'You were hysterical,' he said. 'It was the only way to shut you up. I'm sorry, Em. Does it hurt?'

'Agony,' I said, closing my eyes. A flood of vindictiveness warmed my blood.

'Let's have a look,' he said.

'Don't come near me,' I hissed.

He put a hand under my chin and forced my face up.

'Poor Em,' he said shaking his head. 'What a brute I am.'

'You should be more careful in future,' I said.

'I will, I will,' he said getting to his feet. He looked the picture of contrition. 'And next time don't add so much ochre. Bruises don't usually go yellow till the second day.'

I opened my mouth, shut it again, and started to giggle. I giggled till the tears, and the bruise, ran down my cheeks, until Rory started laughing too.

After that I slept for most of the day. When I woke up, Rory was painting and it was dark outside.

'What time is it?'

'About six.'

Six o'clock – suddenly I wondered what had happened to Finn.

'Did anyone ring?' I asked.

Rory had his back to me. There was a pause, then he said nastily, 'Your boyfriend did telephone about half an hour ago. I told him you were asleep. I'm just going down to the village for some cigarettes,' he added. 'Don't start getting out of bed, or making a bolt for it. I'd track you down in no time, and if you put me to the bother, you wouldn't find me in a very nice mood.'

Chapter Twenty-seven

As soon as he'd gone, I leapt out of bed and rang the hospital. Finn sounded relieved to hear me, but somehow detached.

'Are you OK, darling?'

'I'm fine,' I lied.

'Rory said you were asleep.'

'I was – but, oh, Finn, he's as touchy as gunpowder. I do need you – can't you come over later?'

'I can't, lovie, some of those poor sods from the petrol tanker are in pretty bad shape.'

'Oh, God.' Why did Finn always make me feel slightly ignoble? 'What a horrible, self-centred little bitch I am. I'd forgotten all about them.'

'I hadn't forgotten about you,' said Finn, then someone said something in the background. 'Look, darling, I've got to go. I'll try and come and see you tomorrow.'

The receiver clicked. At that moment Rory walked through the front door and stood in the doorway looking murderous.

'Have you gone quite mad?' he said softly. 'Standing in a howling draught when you're supposed to be in bed? Who were you talking to?'

'Coco. I was just letting her know I'm home.'

'She happens to be in London,' said Rory acidly.

He walked towards me, put his hands on my shoulders, and gazed down at me for a minute. The fury seemed to die out of his eyes.

'Look,' he said, 'you think you're hung up on Finn, but he isn't the answer for you. He's married to his work, always has been. He's a man with no nonsense about him,' and for a minute his face softened. 'And you're a chick with an awful lot of nonsense about you, Em. Now go and get into bed and I'll bring you something to eat.'

I went back to bed and thought about Finn – but at the back of my mind, like an insistent tune, the thought kept repeating itself: if Finn had really loved me, he'd never have let me leave the hospital. He'd have whisked me back to his flat. Rory didn't love me at all, he loved Marina but even so, he'd been utterly single-minded about getting me home and keeping me there. I felt very confused and uncertain of my feelings. I wanted my mother.

Next morning the telephone rang. 'That was your Doctor friend,' said Rory when he'd put the receiver down. 'He's coming round to see you in half an hour.' He went back to his easel, rummaging noisily about for a tube of burnt sienna that he'd mislaid. Finally he gave up looking and poured himself a drink and started painting.

I was dying to go and tart up for Finn. Surreptitiously I levered myself out of bed.

'Where are you going?' said Rory, without turning round.

'To the loo,' I said.

'Again?' said Rory. 'You've just been.'

'I've got a bit of an upset stomach,' I said, sliding towards the door.

'I should have thought it was hardly necessary, then, to take your bag with you,' said Rory.

'Oh,' I said, blushing and putting my bag on the table.

In the bathroom there was nothing to do my face with. I washed and took the shine off my nose with some of Rory's talcum powder, and tidied my hair with Walter Scott's brush. I got back into bed. Rory was still painting ferociously. Very cautiously I eased my bag off the table and just as cautiously opened it. Of course, my bottle of Arpège was at the bottom. I'd scrabbled my way down there, managed to unscrew the top, and was just about to empty some over my wrists when Rory turned round and my bag, plus all its contents and the unstoppered scent bottle, fell with an appalling crash to the floor.

Rory was not amused. We were in the middle of a full-dress row when Finn rang the doorbell. Rory went to let him in. I shoved the bag and all its contents under the bed. The whole room stank of scent like a brothel.

Finn came in, looking boot-faced, but he smiled

when he saw me. Rory went and stood with his back to the fire, his eyes moving from Finn to me.

'All right, Rory, I won't be long,' said Finn dismissively, and picked up my wrist.

'I'll stay if you don't mind,' said Rory.

'Well I do,' I snapped. 'I feel like a biology lesson surrounded by medical students with you both in here.'

'I'll turn my back if you like,' said Rory, 'but keep your thieving hands off her, Doctor,' and he gazed out of the window, whistling Mozart.

'How are you feeling?' said Finn gently. 'Are you eating all right?'

'Like a horse,' said Rory.

'I am not,' I snapped. I grabbed Finn's hand.

'No need to feel Finn's pulse, Emily,' said Rory.

'Oh shut up,' I said.

Finn was a bit like a dignified cart-horse with a couple of mongrels rowing between his legs.

'It's not fair,' I said to Rory afterwards. 'Look at the way you and Marina carry on.'

'We're not talking about me and Marina,' said Rory, his eyes glittering with strain and exasperation. Walter Scott was noisily eating a coat-hanger in the corner.

'Walter thinks your behaviour is appalling,' I said, 'and he knows all about dogs in the manger.'

Chapter Twenty-eight

A week went by. I corrected the proofs of the catalogue for Rory's exhibition. He was painting frantically; wild, swirling, self-absorbed canvases of savage intensity: babies with no arms or legs, feeling their way into life; the agonized features of women giving birth. They were ghastly, hideous paintings but of staggering power. For the first time it occurred to me that Rory might have minded my losing the baby.

He was like a mine-field: one would inadvertently tread on him and he'd explode and smoulder for hours. He was always worse after the times Finn came to see me.

Each time I found Finn increasingly more remote. I couldn't even talk to him because Rory stayed in the room all the time, scowling. It was horribly embarrassing.

Then one night I woke up to find Rory standing by the bed. The fire was dying in the grate. Outside the window the sea gleamed like a python.

'W-what's the matter?' I said nervously.

'I've finished the last painting.'

I sat up sleepily. 'How clever you are. Have you been working all night?'

He nodded. There were great black smudges under his eyes.

'You must be exhausted.'

'A bit. I thought we ought to celebrate.'

He poured champagne into two glasses.

'What time is it?' I said.

'About five-thirty.'

I took a gulp of champagne. It was icy cold and utterly delicious.

'We ought to be sitting on a bench in a rose garden, after a Common Ball,' I said with a giggle. 'You in an evening shirt all covered in my lipstick, and me in a bra-strap dinner frock and a string of pearls.'

He laughed and sat down on the bed. Suddenly I was as jumpy as a cat in his presence – it was as if I were a virgin and he and I had never been to bed together.

He leaned forward and brushed a strand of hair back from my forehead – and it happened. Shocks, rockets, warning bells, the lot, and I knew, blindly, that the old magic was working and I was utterly hooked on him again. Emily the pushover – lying in the gutter with a lion standing over her.

Rory, however, seemed unaware of the chemical change that had taken place in me.

'Oughtn't you to get some sleep?' I said.

'I've got to pack up the canvases,' he said. 'Buster's taking them down to London in his plane.' Then he said, not looking at me, 'He's giving me a lift to Edinburgh.'

Panic swept over me. It was Thursday. Marina's singing lesson day. Oh, God, oh, God, Rory was obviously going to meet her.

'What are you going to Edinburgh for?' I said in a frozen voice.

'To see an American about an exhibition in New York. And a couple of press boys want to talk to me about the London exhibition.'

'When are you coming back?' I said.

'Tonight. My mother's giving a party for my aunt. She's arriving from Paris this evening – you're invited. I think you should come. They're pretty amazing, my aunt and my mother, when they get together. It'd do you good to get out.'

I lay back in bed trying to stop myself crying. Rory bent over and kissed me on the forehead.

'Try and get some more sleep,' he said.

Chapter Twenty-nine

Mrs Mackie, our daily woman, came to look after me while he was away. Her gossiping nearly drove me insane. I washed my hair and shut myself away in the studio to get away from her.

Suddenly there was a knock on the door.

'Someone to see you,' said Mrs Mackie.

And Marina walked in.

I felt weak with relief, as though a great thorn had been pulled out of my side. So Rory hadn't gone to Edinburgh to see her. I wanted to fling my arms round her neck.

'Hello,' I said, grinning from ear to ear.

She seemed shattered by the warmth of my reception.

'Are you going to Coco's party tonight? Hamish wants to, but I'm not sure if I can face it.'

'Oh, I am,' I said, suddenly feeling I wanted to sing from the rooftops. 'It should be a giggle – if Coco's sister's anything like her.'

Marina looked terrible. Her eyes were hidden behind huge amber sunglasses, her face chalky. She looked like someone who was shaking off gastric 'flu.

'Are you all right?' I said suddenly, feeling sorry for her.

'Not very,' she said. 'I'm suffering from a broken heart. Can I have a drink?'

I gave her a huge slug of Rory's whisky. She looked at the golden liquid for a minute, then said: 'Has Rory said anything about me?'

I shook my head.

'Oh, God.' She put her head in her hands. 'I've spent days and days waiting for the Master to ring, but the Master did not ring. He obviously doesn't wish to avail himself of the service.'

'Are you still . . . well, crazy about him?'

'Of course I am!' she screamed, her eyes suddenly wild. 'And he's crazy about me. Nothing will ever cure that.'

I didn't flinch – I was making great strides in self-control these days.

'He's crazy about me, but he feels guilty about you losing the baby. He thinks you've had a lousy deal, so he's got to grit his teeth and try and make a go of it.'

'Charming,' I said, combing and combing my wet hair. She took off her dark glasses. Her eyes were suddenly alight with malevolence.

'Look, you don't love Rory a millionth as much as I do. You wouldn't be playing around with Finn if you did. Finn's crazy about you, and he's a much better proposition than Rory is, he's straight and utterly dependable. You're not tricky enough for Rory, he needs someone who can play him at his own game. You drive him round the bend.'

'It's absolutely mutual,' I said acidly.

'All you've got to do is go to Finn,' said Marina.

'Why doesn't he come and take me away?' I said. 'He's got a car.'

'Because he's had a rough time; he's had one broken marriage, and when he wanted you to leave Rory before you wouldn't go. He wants you to come of your own free will.'

'How idealistic,' I said, sulkily. 'For someone who throws his weight around as much as Finn does, he's very diffident when it comes to sex.'

'He doesn't want to go through hell again, he's got the hospital to consider, and if you don't hurry, Dr Barrett will snap him up. Anyway, can't you realize that if Rory wasn't my brother, he'd drop you like a hot coal?'

Suddenly her face crumpled and she burst into tears. 'I can't stand Hamish any more,' she sobbed. 'You don't know what it's like waking up to that awful old face on the pillow every morning.'

I turned away with a sense of utter weariness. I felt as though I'd been struggling for hours up a hill, and just as I reached the top, my hold had given way and I was pitching headlong into darkness.

After she'd gone, I told Mrs Mackie to go home. I couldn't stand her chatter any more.

Half an hour later, Finn's car drew up outside. I watched him get out and lock it. What the hell did he have to lock it for round here, I thought irritably. There was no-one to pinch any dangerous drugs, except a few sheep.

'Go away,' I said miserably to Finn, refusing to open the door.

'Five minutes,' he said.

'What for?' I said.

'I don't like unfinished business.'

'Is there unfinished business?'

'Come on, stop messing about, let me in.'

'Oh all right,' I said, sulkily, opening the door. He followed me into the drawing-room.

'Do you want a drink?' I said.

'No, I want you,' he ran his hands through his hair, 'I haven't been able to get you on your own since Rory took over.' He looked almost as bad as Marina. Deep lines were entrenched around his mouth and his eyes. He seemed to have aged ten years in as many days.

'You haven't tried very hard,' I said.

'I've been run off my feet – two men from the petrol ship died last night, another early this morning.'

'Oh I'm so sorry,' I said, horrified, 'did they suffer a lot?'

'Yep,' said Finn. 'It hasn't been very pleasant at the hospital – in fact it's been hell.'

'Did you get any extra help from the mainland?' I said.

'I've got another doctor arriving this evening – at least it'll give Jackie a break, she's been marvellous.'

'I'm sure she has,' I said. 'Oh dear, she's far more suitable for you than I am.'

'Maybe she is,' said Finn, 'but it happens to be you that I love. You certainly need more looking after than she does; what the hell are you wandering about with bare feet and wet hair for?' He picked up a towel. 'Come on, I'll dry it for you.'

'No, it'll go all fluffy.' Finn took no notice. Christ, he rubbed hard.

'I won't have any scalp left,' I grumbled.

After that, the inevitable happened and I ended up in his arms, and I must confess that I did like kissing him very much. It was one of the great all-time pleasures, like smoked salmon and Brahms' second piano concerto. Then I started getting nervous that Rory might walk in, so I wriggled out of his grasp.

'Who told you Rory was away?' I said.

'Marina did.'

'She has been busy,' I said. 'She was here earlier telling me how much she and Rory still love each other, and how noble Rory had been coming back to me.'

'Rory,' said Finn, kicking a log on the fire, 'has never done anything noble in his life. This little display of territorial imperative is sheer bloody-mindedness because he doesn't want *me* to get you. It's only *me* he's jealous about. Did he ever give

195

a damn when Calen Macdonald made a pass at you?'

'No,' I said, plunging back into the depths of gloom.

'Why don't you leave him? You know how much I want you to.'

'The downward path is easy,' I said, 'but there's no turning back. When your dear, scheming sister was telling me how mad Rory is about her, it hurt me so much I couldn't speak, but when she started dropping dark hints about you and Doctor Barrett, it irritated me but it didn't tear me in pieces at all . . . Q.E.D. I love Rory, not you.' I suddenly felt a great sense of loss. 'I'm wildly attracted to you, physically,' I said, 'I expect I always will be, but I'm stuck with loving Rory.'

'Even if he doesn't love you?'

I nodded. I played my last card:

'The only way it might work is if we went away together, away from Irasa, and Rory and Marina, and all those associations – but that would mean your leaving the hospital.'

'Darling, I can't abandon it at this stage,' said Finn. 'You know I can't.'

I could see the pain starting in his eyes. I went over and put my arms round his neck, breathing in his strong, male solidarity.

'Oh Finn,' I whispered, 'I'm so sorry it's not you.'

Chapter Thirty

All in all I didn't feel in a very festive state for Coco's party. Numb misery would have just about summed it up. Rory had noticed my red eyes when he got home, and demanded to know what was the matter. I'd refused to tell him, and he'd got extremely bad tempered.

I was wearing a very sexy red dress, but in my current condition I felt about as sexy as a pillar-box.

'At least it matches your eyes,' said Rory.

Coco's party was the usual noisy success, but everyone seemed even more anxious to get drunk than usual.

'My sister arrives later,' Coco told me. 'She says she is bringing me a surprise. I think I am too old to be surprised by anything, but perhaps it will be something that amuses Buster.'

Marina was wearing a beautiful white dress: everything about her shimmered and glimmered softly as though the material had been woven of candle beams. But inside it she looked like a stricken masquerader. Hamish was there, too, looking dreadfully old and ill.

I hadn't seen him since the night he told me Rory and Marina were brother and sister.

Rory was drinking steadily and talking to Buster about fishing – Buster was in a very good temper, having landed a huge salmon that afternoon.

I was being the death and soul of the party.

About ten o'clock, after supper, a crowd of us were in a little room off the hall, playing roulette. Rory was winning, Hamish was losing heavily. Buster was still talking about his salmon. 'Amazing fish, the salmon,' he said, placing four chips on Rouge. 'They live for years in salt water, and then always come back to the same freshwater spot to breed.'

'Not surprising,' said Marina, and she looked at Rory and laughed. 'As you'd know, Buster, if you'd ever suffered the agony of making love in salt water.'

'I really thought the bugger had got away,' said Buster, not listening at all.

'Not surprising,' said Rory, 'if he saw you hauling on the other end of the line.'

Then, just as there was a pause in play, and Buster was raking in counters, Hamish looked at Rory.

'I hope you've been keeping a pretty close guard on your wife lately,' he said.

Rory stopped in the middle of lighting a cigarette.

'Shut up, Hamish,' I snapped.

'Hush, darling,' Rory put his hand on my arm. 'Hamish is about to explain himself.'

'All I'm saying,' said Hamish, flashing his false teeth evilly, 'is that patients often fall in love with their doctors, and it's nice to know I'm not the only cuckold in Irasa.'

His words brought an uneasy silence.

'Belt up, Hamish,' said Buster. 'You don't know what you're saying.'

'Oh, I do, Buster, old chap. All I'm saying to Rory is that next time he goes to Edinburgh, and my wife disappears to join him, he should realize that while he's away, pretty Mrs Balniel will be amusing herself with Dr Maclean.'

'That's not true,' I squeaked.

'Are you going to take that back?' said Rory through clenched teeth.

'No, dear boy, I'm not. Your wife is as big a whore . . .'

He got no further. Rory had chucked his drink into Hamish's face.

'And that's a waste of good whisky,' he said.

Hamish, whisky dripping from his face, made a lunge at Rory.

Buster pulled him off.

The doorbell rang noisily, bringing us back to our senses.

'Buster, Rory,' shrieked Coco from the hall, 'I think it must be Marcelle.'

'Excuse me,' said Buster, and hurried out.

Hamish wiped the whisky off his face. I dared not look at Rory or Marina.

The next minute, Coco swept into the room with her sister, Marcelle.

We all tried to act normally and everyone kissed everyone on both cheeks. Marcelle was not as pretty as Coco, younger and brassier, but pretty high voltage all the same.

She said, with a touch of malice: 'I've brought you your surprise, chérie. He's putting the car away and feeling a little shy, too.'

'Why don't you go and get him, Buster?' said Coco.

Buster trotted out obediently.

'Who can it be?' said Coco excitedly. 'I have so many skeletons in the wardrobe.'

I'd had my share of surprises, too. I was still shaking from Hamish's accusations. I sat down on the sofa. The next moment Buster came through the door. For once he'd lost his superb indolence. He looked shattered. He went up to Coco.

'Darling,' he whispered. 'This is going to be something of a shock.'

'I hope it's a nice one,' said Coco, patting her curls and arranging her breasts in the low-cut black dress. Someone else stood behind Buster in the door, a tall thin figure.

Alerted by everyone's faces, Buster swung round.

'For Christ's sake,' he snapped. 'I told you to wait.'

I watched, fascinated, as the man came through the door. He had unruly black hair streaked with grey, high cheek bones, formidable, contemptuous black eyes above grey pouches, and a haughty thin-lipped mouth. He was dressed theatrically in a black cloak with a gold earring hanging from one ear. He looked around slowly, taking everyone in. He must have been at least fifty – but he was still sensationally attractive. And I knew positively that I'd met him somewhere before.

There was a pause, then Coco turned as white as a sheet. 'Alexei,' she said in a frozen tone. Then she gave a strange little laugh that was almost a sob, and running towards him, flung her arms round his neck.

The odd thing was the silence. Everyone in the room looked stunned.

'You're still very beautiful, Coco,' Alexei said softly. 'How did I ever let you go?'

Coco seemed to recover herself.

'I was not rich enough for you,' she said un-romantically.

'You haven't been properly introduced to my husband, have you, Alexei?' said Coco. 'Alexei was a great boyfriend of mine before I married Hector,' she said.

'So it seems,' said Buster.

'I seem to have stumbled on a little family gathering,' said the stranger with amusement.

Oh, where had I seen that arrogant, equivocal smile before?

'You must also meet my son, Rory,' said Coco.

Rory got to his feet.

Very carefully, they looked each other up and down.

I looked from Rory to the stranger. The resemblance was unmistakable.

'Did you say Alexei was a boyfriend of yours before you married my father, or afterwards?' Rory said softly.

Coco shrugged her shoulders, 'Well, a bit of both, darling.'

Alexei turned to Rory. 'Your mother and I were very much in love but, alas, we neither of us had any money. So she married Hector, and I, alas, martyred in the arms of . . .'

'A fat American heiress,' said Coco.

Then Rory started to laugh. He got a drink and raised it to Hector's portrait, kilted and bristling, over the fire. 'So the old bastard wasn't my father after all,' he said, and turning to Alexei, 'I do hope you don't expect me to call you Daddy?'

Coco smiled. 'You do not mind, chérie?'

Rory shook his head. 'As long as his references are all right.'

Alexei grinned in genuine amusement. 'Oh, they're extremely good, my dear. I'm Russian; white, of course, and can trace my ancestry back to centuries before Peter the Great.'

His glance wandered in my direction. He had exactly the same way of stripping off all one's clothes that Rory had.

'This is Rory's wife,' said Coco.

Alexei sighed and bowed over my hand. 'What a pity,' he said, 'I suppose that puts her out of bounds?'

'I wouldn't let that worry you,' I said in a shaking voice. 'Incest has never deterred anyone in this house.'

I'll never understand any of them, I thought hopelessly. Only Marina was beginning to generate a fitting amount of emotion.

The next moment she had rushed up to Rory and flung her arms round his neck.

'Don't you see, darling?' she cried wildly. 'That lets you and me off the hook.'

The room swam before me.

Chapter Thirty-one

The next moment I blacked out. I remember coming to and seeing a sea of faces and hearing Rory shouting at everyone to get out of the way and give me some air.

'She looks terrible,' said Coco. 'Are you all right, *mon ange*?'

'She got up too soon,' said Buster.

'She ought to see someone,' said Coco.

'I can see at least ten people already,' I joked feebly.

'Shall I call Finn?' said Marina.

'No,' snapped Rory, 'that's the last thing she needs,' and picking me up, he carried me upstairs.

'You'll rupture yourself,' I grumbled, as he stumbled on the top step. Thank God I'd lost some weight in hospital.

Rory kicked the door of the best guest room open. A fire was blazing in the grate. The purple-flowered sheets of the bed were turned down. The scent of freesias filled the room.

'But it's all ready for Marcelle,' I said feebly.

'She can sleep somewhere else,' said Rory, depositing me on the bed. He started to undo the zip of my dress.

'I'll do it,' I stammered, leaping away. He looked at me, frowning.

'Do you hate me so much you can't even bear me to touch you?'

'No – I mean . . .'

'What do you mean?' The tension was unbearable.

'I can't explain.' He shrugged his shoulders.

'All right, if that's the way you want it. I'll get you a couple of my mother's sleeping pills.'

I sat down on the bed, burying my face in my hands. I felt sick. How could I explain to him that I couldn't bear him to touch me because if he did, I'd only collapse, gibbering with lust, telling him I couldn't live without him, that I loved him – all the things he hated.

Coco's sleeping pills must have been very strong. It was mid-day when I woke up. The sun was streaming through the curtains, everything was quiet, except for a persistent thrush, and the occasional click of Buster hitting a captive golf-ball in the garden.

The fire had been re-lit in the grate. The scent of freesias was stronger than ever. Walter Scott lay sprawled across my feet. It was such a pretty room. For a moment I wallowed in the voluptuous euphoria created by the sleeping pills, then, bit by bit, the events of the last night came filtering back. Coco's sister arriving and then that glorious Russian turning out to be Rory's father, and Rory not being Marina's brother after all, and there being nothing now to stop them getting married – and having hordes of ravishing black-eyed, red-haired children or ravishing blue-eyed, black-haired children. Oh, God, God, God, I writhed on the pillow – a bad business paid only with agony.

What the hell was I to do next? The last month had been difficult certainly, Rory and I living together with no sex, but at least we'd had a few laughs, and I felt somehow that even if he didn't love me in the white-hot way he loved Marina, he was making very real efforts to make a go of it. Then Marina's words of yesterday came back to me: 'If he weren't my brother, he'd drop you like a hot coal.'

I lay feeling suicidal for a bit, then got up and drew back the curtains. It was a marvellous day, the sea sparkling, the larches waving their pale green branches against an angelically blue sky. I felt the sun warming my hair and smoothing away the marks of the sheets on my skin.

Buster, hearing the curtains draw, looked up. I moved out of range and examined my body in the mirror. The only advantage about being miserable is you do lose weight. For a minute I forgot my gloom and admired my flat stomach and my ribs, then I sucked in my cheeks, and putting on a haughty model's face, stood up on my toes.

'Very nice,' said a voice at the door, 'you'll make the gatefold of *Playboy* yet.' It was Rory. I gave a squeak of embarrassment and grabbed a towel to cover myself. 'Don't,' he said, shutting the door. He looked extremely pleased with himself. I wondered, with a flash of despair, if he'd spent the night celebrating with Marina.

'You look better,' he said, coming towards me. I backed away.

'Oh for God's sake, Em, stop behaving like a frightened horse.'

He was wearing a dark blue sweater, and an old pair of paint-stained jeans; his hair was ruffled by the wind: he looked so unspeakably handsome, I felt my entrails go liquid. I lowered my eyes in case he read the absolutely blatant desire there. I wanted him so much I had to turn away and jump back into bed, pulling the sheets up to my neck.

'That's a good girl,' said Rory. 'It seems a pity to get up on such a lovely day.'

'Where is everyone?' I asked.

'Wandering around the house in various stages of undress, groaning about their hangovers.' He sat down on the bed and lit a cigarette. 'Do you still feel sick, does the smoke worry you?'

I shook my head in surprise, fancy Rory bothering to ask that.

'How are you getting on, adjusting to your new – er – father?' I baulked on the word.

Rory grinned. 'I quite like him, but he's an old

phoney; he's already tried to borrow money off me, but then my mother always did have frightful taste in men. I'm very glad he didn't bring me up, I'd have been cooling my heels in Broadmoor by now.'

'Is he as grand as he makes out?' I said.

'I don't think so, he looks degenerate enough, but I don't believe those claims about tracing his ancestry back to Peter the Great. It does appear in fact that I've been born on the wrong side of an awful lot of blankets. Do you mind having an illegitimate husband?'

'Do *you* mind?' I said cagily.

'Not at all, I never understood how Hector could be related to me anyway. His favourite painter was Peter Scott. There's only one slight problem now to tax the ingenuity of the family solicitor. Have I any right any more to Hector's money?'

'Are you worried about it?'

'Not particularly, I quite like the thought of starving in a garret.' He shot me a glance under his eyelashes. 'How about you?'

'I haven't tried it,' I said carefully. 'How's your mother taking it?'

'Medium. I think she's a bit put out. Buster and Alexei have taken to each other like drakes to water, great bounders think alike I suppose. Alexei, like all foreigners, has a great reverence for English upper-class institutions. His ambition, like Buster's, is to murder as much wildlife as he can. He's so heartbroken the grouse shooting season is over that

Buster has promised to take him pigeon shooting this afternoon.'

'Are you going?' I said.

'I might – for a laugh. So my mother is rather irritated about the whole thing. She's not gaining an ex-lover, she's losing a husband. Alexei is between marriages at the moment, I think he and Buster might do very well together.'

'But he's old enough to be Buster's father,' I said.

'Probably is, if I know that lot,' said Rory. I burst out laughing. Rory took my hand. 'You haven't laughed much lately, Em. I think we ought to have a talk.'

I snatched my hand away, 'People always say that,' I said in a trembling voice, 'when they're about to say something awful.'

'I've made you very unhappy since I married you, haven't I?' said Rory. 'I'm sorry, you must have had a pretty bloody six months.'

Panic swept over me. 'Come on,' he said in an exaggeratedly gentle voice, 'come here.' He held out his arms to me.

'No,' I said desperately, 'no, no, no.'

I knew exactly what he was about to say, that he'd made me so unhappy I obviously didn't want to stay married to him any longer, so why didn't we have an amicable divorce? If he touched me, I knew I'd cry.

'Is it that bad?' he said.

I nodded, biting my lip.

'I gather Finn Maclean was round to see you

yesterday,' he said in a flat voice. 'Are you still hooked on him – come on, I want the truth.'

I felt defeated, my eyes filled with tears. There was a knock on the door. 'Go away,' howled Rory. In walked Finn. 'My God,' exploded Rory, 'why the hell can't you ever leave us alone? What do you mean by barging in here, who the hell asked you?'

'I've come to have a look at Emily,' said Finn.

'You've had a bloody sight too many looks at Emily recently,' said Rory.

'She happens to be a patient of mine.'

'Among other things,' said Rory. 'She's perfectly all right.'

'She looks it,' said Finn. He bent down to stroke Walter Scott who thumped his tail noisily on the floor.

'And stop sucking up to my dog,' snarled Rory.

'Oh, please,' I said, 'leave Finn and me for a few minutes.'

Rory scowled at both of us. 'All right,' he said, going towards the door, 'but if you put a finger wrong, Finn, I'll report you to the medical council and get you struck off the register.' And he slammed the door so hard, all the windows rattled.

Finn raised an eyebrow. 'What was that little tantrum in aid of?'

'He was trying to give me the sack,' I said miserably. 'And you interrupted him. You've heard that his real father's turned up?'

Finn nodded.

'So there's nothing to stop Rory and Marina now.'

'It's not going to be as easy as that, there's Hamish to be considered. I doubt if he'll give Marina a divorce.'

'It's funny,' I said, feeling very ashamed of myself, 'none of us ever thinks of Hamish, do we?'

Finn gave me some tranquillizers. 'Look,' he said, 'I'm off to a conference in Glasgow this afternoon. I'd cancel it, but I've got to speak. I'm not too happy about the current situation. Marina's in a highly overwrought state. So, obviously, is Rory, and I'm worried about Hamish. I want you to stay in bed today. I'll be staying at the Kings Hotel tonight, don't hesitate to ring me if you need me. Here's the telephone number.' He dropped a kiss on the top of my head. 'Don't look so miserable, little one, things will sort themselves out.'

Knocking back tranquillizers like Smarties, I decided to disregard Finn's advice and get up. When I finally made it downstairs, I found a noisy and drunken lunch had just finished. The debris of wine glasses, napkins and cigar butts still lay on the dining-room table. Buster was bustling about organizing his pigeon shoot. I went into the kitchen and opened a tin of Pedigree Chum for Walter. Then wandered into the drawing-room where I found Alexei well entrenched, chewing on a large cigar, drinking port and reading a book called *The Grouse in Health and in Disease.*

'Ah, my enchanting daughter-in-law,' he said, getting to his feet and kissing my hand with a flourish. Oh God, I hoped my fingers didn't smell of Pedigree Chum. 'Come and sit down,' he patted a rather small space on the sofa beside him, 'and tell me about yourself.'

Predictably I couldn't think of anything to say, but Alexei had obviously had enough to drink for it not to matter a scrap.

'Coco tells me you lost a baby recently – I am so sorry – you must have been very disappointed. You must have another one – as soon as you're strong again. You and Rory would have beautiful children.' It was not a subject I cared to dwell on.

'Do you have lots of children yourself?' I said.

'Yes, I think so, several that I know about and several that I probably don't, but none, I think, as talented as Rory. I have been looking at his paintings this morning. I am proud of my new son, he is a very good-looking boy, I think.'

'Yes, he is,' I said wistfully.

'And not unlike me, I think,' said Alexei with satisfaction. He got up. 'I must go and change for the shooting.'

'But it'll be dark in a couple of hours,' I said.

'We wait till dusk and catch the pigeons as they come home to roost,' he said.

'Poor things,' I said. 'Where's Rory?'

'Gone to fetch his gun. Hamish is coming too.' Suddenly, in spite of the centrally heated fug of the house, I felt icy cold. I didn't like the idea of that cast of characters going shooting.

Alexei went up to change. I turned on the television and watched a steeplechase. It all looked so bright green and innocent one couldn't really believe those horses falling at the fences were really hurting themselves.

A few minutes later, Rory arrived with Walter Scott. 'Who told you to get up?' he asked angrily. 'You look frightful.'

'I thought I might come and watch you all shooting,' I said.

'Absolutely not,' snapped Rory. 'You're supposed to rest – according to *your* doctor. Go back upstairs at once.'

At that moment Buster walked in, looking ludicrously like a French tart in rubber thigh boots and an extraordinary hat with a veil.

'Time's getting on, Rory,' he said, 'we ought to take up our positions at least an hour before dusk.'

'Is he getting married to Alexei already?' I said.

Rory laughed: 'It's supposed to stop the pigeons seeing his face when they fly over – a pity he doesn't wear it all the time. Come on,' he whistled to Walter Scott.

'Rory,' I said. He turned in the doorway. 'Be careful,' I said.

'Don't worry,' he said. 'It's all gun and no fear.'

I met Coco coming down the stairs.

''Ullo bébé, how are you, I am fed up. I 'ope the presence of Alexei would make Buster jealous, and spend less time on his horrible bloody sports, but it only makes 'im worse. I like to have a good sleep in the afternoon, but what is the point if there is no-one to sleep with you? So Marcelle and I decided to go over to the mainland. You will be all right, *mon ange*?'

'Of course,' I said.

I tried to sleep but I was in much too uptight a state. I heard voices outside and crept to the window to see them go off. Poor Hamish looked iller than ever. Alexei was laughing at some joke of Buster's. Walter Scott, who was thoroughly over-excited by the whole proceedings, suddenly decided to mount Hamish's red setter bitch. Hamish went mad and rushed over and started kicking Walter in the ribs in a frenzy. Walter started howling and Rory turned on Hamish in fury. I couldn't hear what he was saying, but Hamish went absolutely spare with rage. I could see the white of his knuckles as his hands clenched on his gun. Then Buster came over and said something and they all set off, their boots ringing on the drive.

They crossed the burn and took the narrow, winding path up to the pine woods. I thought of the pigeons coming home after a long day to face the music: tomorrow they would be strung up as corpses in the larder, their destination pigeon pie.

I took more tranquillizers and tried to sleep, but it

214

was impossible. I tried to read, Coco had left some magazines by the bed. I read my horoscope, which was lousy. Rory's horoscope said he was going to have a good week for romance, blast him, but should be careful of unforeseen danger towards the weekend. I should never have let him go shooting.

An explosion of guns in the distance made me jump nervously. Then I heard a crunch of wheels on the gravel and looked out of the window again. It was Marina, Miss Machiavelli herself. She parked her blue car in front of the house and switched off the engine, then combed her hair, powdered her nose, and put on more scent – the conniving bitch. God, how I hated her.

She got out of the car, fragile in a huge sheepskin coat and brown boots, her red hair streaming in the breeze, and set off down the track the guns had taken.

No wonder Rory had been so insistent about my staying in bed and keeping out of his way. Drawn by some terrible fascination to see what they were getting up to, I got up, put on an old sheepskin coat of Coco's and set off after her.

The guns popped in the distance, like some far-off firework party. It was getting dark, the fir trees beetled darkly, a rabbit scuttled over the dead leaves, frightening the life out of me. The sweat was rising on my forehead, my breath coming in great gasps. I ran on, ducking to avoid overhanging branches. There was the ADDERS – PLEASE KEEP OUT sign Buster had put up to frighten off tourists. I could hear voices now; the colour was going out of the woods; in the distance the sea was darkening to gun metal.

Suddenly I rounded a corner and, to my relief, saw Buster's gamekeeper, then Marina's red hair, and the guns strung out in a ring; Buster still wearing that ludicrous veil, Alexei next to him, then Rory, then Hamish, with Marina standing between them, but slightly behind. She was lighting one cigarette from another. I hoped they wouldn't see me, then I stepped on a twig and she and Rory looked round. He looked absolutely furious. Buster smiled at me, waving and indicating to me to stay quiet. Walter Scott sat beside Rory, quivering with excitement, trying to look grown up. Marina tiptoed back and stood beside me. On closer inspection she didn't look so hot, her skin pale and mottled, her eyes sunken and bloodshot. Even so, there was plenty of the old dash about her.

'I thought you were at death's door,' she said. 'It's been quite exciting, Alexei has already tried to shoot a couple of sheep and nearly killed Hamish – I wish he'd tried harder.'

'What are they waiting for?' I asked.

'The pigeons,' she said, 'they're late back. I had the most cataclysmic row with Hamish last night,' she said, lowering her voice. 'I ended up throwing most of the silver at him. We started at four o'clock in the morning and went on till just before he came out. This is half-time, I ought to be sucking oranges and thinking what to do in the second half. He said I behaved atrociously last night,' she went on, her eyes glittering wildly, 'and that he absolutely refuses to divorce me. Has Rory spoken to you?' she said, suddenly tense.

'He tried to this morning,' I hissed, 'but your dear brother walked in in the middle.'

'The trouble is,' whispered Marina, 'that Rory feels frightfully guilty about you because everything's worked out for him, now he can marry me. If you went off with Finn it would make things much easier for everyone.'

'I don't want to go off with Finn,' I said, my voice rising. 'What the hell do you think you're doing, riding roughshod over everyone's lives, don't you ever think that Hamish and I might have feelings?'

Marina turned her great headlamp eyes on me: 'I'd never hang around being a bore to a man who couldn't stand me – I've got too much pride, you obviously haven't.'

'Shut up you two,' said Buster.

We were silent but the whole forest must have heard my heart thudding.

Then suddenly the pigeons came sailing over the view over the pine tops, and with a deafening crash the guns went off. It was like being in the middle of a thunderstorm, except that the sky was raining pigeons. The deafening fusillade lasted about three minutes.

Some of the birds escaped unscathed, others came down directly. The guns charged about looking for booty. Dogs circled, cursed by their masters. Alexei stood proudly with two birds in each hand. There were congratulations and verdicts. Walter Scott rushed grinning up to me, his mouth full of feathers.

'Must be some more in here,' said Buster, disappearing into the undergrowth. A minute later his great red face appeared and he said in a low voice, 'Rory, come here a minute.' Rory, followed by Walter Scott, went into the undergrowth.

There was a pause, then Rory came out, his face ashen in the half light, shaking like a leaf.

'What's the matter, darling?' Marina ran forward. 'What's happened?'

'It's Hamish,' said Rory. 'There's been an accident. I'm afraid he's blown his brains out.' His face suddenly worked like a small boy about to cry. 'Don't look, Marina, it's horrible.'

Marina gave a scream and rushed into the wood after Buster. Rory disappeared to the right: next moment I heard the sound of retching.

Marina emerged a minute later, her eyes mad with hysteria. 'There, you see,' she screamed at me, 'Rory killed him, he killed him for me, because he thought Hamish wasn't going to let me go. Now who do you think Rory loves?'

'Don't be bloody silly, Marina,' said Buster, coming out of the copse. 'Of course Rory didn't kill him, poor old boy obviously did himself in.'

Rory, having regained his composure, had returned.

'I didn't, Marina,' he said, as she ran forward and collapsed in his arms. 'I swear I didn't.'

'Well, it's my fault then,' she sobbed. 'I told Hamish to do it, I told him how much I loathed and hated him, how much he disgusted me. I goaded him into it. Oh, Rory, Rory, I'll never forgive myself.'

I turned away. I couldn't bear the infinitely tender way he was holding her in his arms, stroking her hair, and telling her everything would be all right. Suddenly there was an unearthly wailing: everyone jumped nervously, then we realized it was Hamish's red setter howling with misery.

'She was the only one,' said Rory, 'who gave a damn for the poor old bugger.'

Chapter Thirty-two

I can't really remember much of getting back.

Rory took me home; he was in a terrible state, shaking like a leaf. He came in and poured a stiff whisky and downed it in one gulp.

'Look, I must go to her.'

I nodded mechanically. 'Yes, of course you must.'

'I'm frightened this will unhinge her; I feel sort of responsible, do you understand?'

'Yes, I do.'

'Do you want to come too?'

I looked at him for the last time, taking in the brown fur rug on the sofa, the yellow cushions, the gold of his corduroy jacket, his dark hair and deathly pale face, the smell of turpentine, the utter despair in my heart. I shook my head, 'I'd rather stay here.'

'I won't be long,' he said, and was gone.

So Hamish had loved Marina after all. What was it that Marina had said that afternoon – that she'd never hang around being a bore to a man who couldn't stand her.

So the game had ended that never should have begun. I'm not a noble character, but I know when I'm licked.

For the second time in two months I packed my suitcase. I had no thought of going to Finn. Finn fancied me, but he didn't really love me. Not as Rory understood love. And now I couldn't have Rory, I didn't want second best.

I left a note.

'Darling,
Hamish has set you and Marina free, now I'm going to do the same. Please be happy and don't try and find me.

Emily.'

Mist swathed the Irasa hills, the lochs lay about them like steel and silver medallions in the moonlight. A small, chill wind whispered among the heather. I walked the narrow track that twisted down the hill to the ferry. I caught the last boat of the day. There was scarcely anyone on it. I stood on deck, and watched the castle and everything I loved in the world getting dimmer and dimmer until they vanished in a mist of tears.

I shall never remember how I got through the next ten days. I went to ground in a shabby London hotel bedroom. I couldn't eat, I couldn't sleep. I just lay dry-eyed on my bed like a wounded animal, shocked by incredulous grief and horror.

I toyed with the idea of going to see my parents, or ringing up Nina, but I couldn't bear the expressions of sympathy, then the whispering, and later, the 'I told you so's', and 'We always knew he was a bad lot', and much later – the 'Pull yourself togethers'. Sooner or later I knew I would have to face up to life, but I hadn't got the courage to get in touch with them yet, nor could I face the bitter disappointment I would feel if Rory hadn't rung them and tried to contact me.

But why should he contact me? He must be blissfully happy now with Marina. The idea of them together rose black and churning. Sometimes I thought I was going mad. Even my unconscious played tricks on me. Every night I dreamed of Rory and woke up in tears. In the street I saw lean, dark, tall men and, heart thumping, would charge forward, shrinking away in horror when I realized it wasn't him.

I hoped I would find it easier as the days went by, but it got much worse. What I hadn't anticipated was going slap into the infinitely bosky lushness of a late London spring. Everything was far further on than it was in Scotland. Outside my bedroom window the new lime-green leaves of the plane trees swung like little cherubs' wings, ice-cream pink cherry trees were dropping their blossom on the long grass. Huge velvety purple irises and bluebells filled the Chelsea gardens. Everywhere, too, there was an atmosphere of sexiness, of sap rising, of pretty girls walking the streets in their new summer dresses, of men whistling at them, of lovers entwined in the park, everything geared to ram home my loss to me.

'He's gone, he's gone, and when thou knowest this thou knowest how dry a cinder this world is.'

The day of the opening of Rory's exhibition came and went. With heroic self-control, I stuck to the hotel and didn't hang around in the coffee bar opposite in the hope of getting a glimpse of him. I couldn't face the anguish of seeing him with Marina.

But next morning I dragged myself up and went out and bought the papers, and crept back to the hotel to read them. The reviews were very mixed: some of the critics loathed the paintings, some adored them, but everyone agreed that a dazzling new talent had arrived. There were also several pictures of Rory looking sulky and arrogant, and impossibly handsome. The Nureyev of the Art world, the gossip columns called him.

I cried half the morning, trying to decide what to do; then the manager presented me with my weekly bill, and I realized I could only just pay it. Next week I should have to get a job.

I had a bath and washed my hair. I looked frightful, like one of those women that wait for the bodies at the pit head – even make-up didn't help much. I can't even make any money as a tart now, I said dismally – I'd have to pay *them*.

When I got to Bond Street, I felt giddy. It struck

me I hadn't eaten for days. I went into a coffee bar and ordered an omelette, but when it arrived I took one bite and thought I was going to throw up. Chucking down a pound I fled into the street. Four doors down, I went up the steps to the agency that used to find me work in the old days. How well I remembered that grey-carpeted, grey-walled, potted-plant world that I hoped I'd abandoned for ever. I started to sweat and tremble.

Audrey Kennaway, the principal, agreed to see me. She greeted me in an immaculate, utterly awful primrose yellow dress and jacket. Her heavily made-up eyes swept over me.

'Well, Emily,' she said in cooing tones, 'it's nice to see you. How are you enjoying your new jet-set life? Are you on your way to Newmarket or the Cannes Film Festival?'

'Actually, neither, I'm looking for a job,' I blurted out.

'A job?' She raised eyebrows plucked to the edge of extinction. 'Surely not, but I thought your hand-some husband was doing so well, he had such a success in the papers this morning.' Her red-nailed fingers drummed on the table.

'That's all over,' I muttered. 'It didn't work out.'

'I'm sorry,' she said. I'm not surprised, I could see her thinking, she's let herself go so much. Her manner had become distinctly chillier.

'There's not a lot of work about at the moment, people are laying off staff everywhere,' she went on.

'Oh dear,' I said feebly. 'In my day, they were always laying on them.'

Audrey Kennaway smiled coolly.

'You'll have to smarten yourself up a bit,' she said.

'I know, I know,' I said. 'I haven't been very well. I used to type a bit, do you remember?' I went on. 'And when I was thin, you sometimes got me television commercials or a bit of modelling. I'm much thinner than that now.'

'I don't think I could find you anything in that field at the moment. Let's see if there's any filing clerk work.' Her long red talons started moving through the cards in a box on her desk. I felt great tears filling my eyes. I struggled to control myself for a minute, then leapt to my feet.

'I'm sorry,' I said, 'I couldn't do a filing job. I can't even file my nails without setting my teeth on edge. It's a mistake for me to have come here. You're quite right, I couldn't hold a job down at the moment. I can't hold down anything.' Bursting into tears, I fled out of the office, down the stairs into the sunshine. Two streets away was Rory's gallery. Gradually, as though pulled by some invisible hand, I was drawn towards it. I went into a chemist's to buy some dark glasses with my last pound. They weren't much help, they hid my red eyes but the tears kept trickling underneath. Slowly I edged down Grafton Street. No. 212, here it was; my knees were knocking together, my throat dry.

There was one of Rory's paintings of the Irasa coast in the window. Two fat women were looking at it.

'I don't go for this modern stuff,' said one.

I entered the gallery, my heart pounding. Then, with a thud of disappointment, I realized Rory wasn't there. I looked around, the paintings looked superb, and so many already had red 'sold' stickers on them. By the desk an American was writing out a cheque to a chinless wonder.

I wandered round the room, proud yet bitterly resentful that people should be able to buy something that was so much a part of Rory.

The chinless wonder, having ditched the American, wandered over.

'Can I help you?' he said.

'I was just looking round,' I said. 'You seem to have sold a lot.'

'We did awfully well yesterday, and we sold four more this morning – not, I may add,' he whispered darkly, 'through any assistance on the artist's part.'

'What do you mean?' I said, startled.

The chinless wonder smoothed his pale gold hair.

'Well, he's talented, I admit, but quite frankly, he's an ugly customer. Doesn't give a damn about the show being a success.'

He put stickers on two more paintings.

'Always thought the fellow was pretty cold-blooded,' he went on. 'Didn't seem to care about anything, but he's certainly cut up at the moment.

Apparently his wife's left him. Can't say I blame her. Only been married six months. He's absolutely devastated. I mean, he was a dead loss at the private view on Thursday. I'd lined up a host of press boys to meet him, and he wouldn't speak to any of them. Just hung around the door, hoping she might turn up.'

I leant against the wall for support.

'D-did you say his wife has just left him?' I said slowly. 'Are you sure it's his wife he's cut up about?'

'Certain,' said the chinless wonder. 'I'll show you a picture of her.'

We moved into a second room, where I steeled myself to confront one of Rory's beautiful voluptuous nude paintings of Marina.

'There she is,' he said, pointing to a small oil opposite the window. I felt my knees go weak, my throat dry – because it was a painting of me in jeans and an old sweater, looking incredibly sad. I never knew that Rory had painted it. Tears stung my eyelids.

'Are you sure that's the one?' I whispered.

'That's her,' said the chinless wonder. 'I mean it's a great painting, but she's not a patch on that gorgeous redhead he was always painting in the nude. Still, I suppose there's no accounting for tastes. I say, are you feeling all right? Would you like to sit down?'

Then he looked at the painting – and at me.

'I say,' he said, absolutely appalled, 'how frightfully

rude of me. That painting – it's you, isn't it? I really didn't mean to be rude.'

'You haven't been,' I said, half laughing, half crying. 'It's the nicest, nicest thing anyone's ever said to me in my life. Do you possibly know where he's staying?'

Chapter Thirty-three

I ran towards the tube station, rocked by conflicting emotions. It was the rush hour. As I battled with the crowds, I tried to calm the turmoil raging inside me. It couldn't be true, it couldn't be true. Then suddenly, as I reached the bottom of the steps, I was absolutely knocked sideways by an ecstatic, whining, black heap leaping up and licking my face, its tail going in a frenzy.

'Walter,' I sobbed, flinging my arms round his neck. 'Oh Walter, where's your master?' I looked up and there was Rory.

'Come here, you bloody dog!' he was shouting from the other side of the crowd. His slit eyes were restless, ranging from one person to another, sliding towards me. Then, as if drawn by the violence of my longing, they fastened on me, and I saw him start in recognition.

I tried to call his name, but the words were strangled in my throat.

'Emily!' he yelled.

The next moment he was fighting his way through the crowd.

'Oh, Emily, Emily, darling,' he said. 'Don't ever run away again.'

And pinning me against the wall, hunching his shoulders against the pressure of the crowd, he began to kiss me greedily, angrily, as tears of love and happiness streaked my face.

After a few minutes I drew away, gasping for breath.

'We can't stay here,' said Rory, and dragged me in my tearful blindness, muttering incoherently, out into the street and across the road to his hotel, where he kissed me all the way up in the lift, utterly oblivious of the lift man. Walter Scott jumped about trying to lick my hands.

'What the bloody hell,' said Rory, as he slammed the bedroom door behind us, 'do you mean by running away like that?' That sounded more like the old Rory. 'I've had the most frightful ten days of my life. And poor Walter,' he went on, 'how do you think he's enjoyed being the victim of a broken home?'

'I didn't think you loved me,' I said, collapsing on to the bed.

'Jes-us,' said Rory, 'I tried to tell you enough times. Didn't I wear myself out trying to fend off that smug bastard Finn Maclean? I nearly put a bullet through him that night I found him kissing you in the corridor at the hospital. And I've been driven absolutely insane with jealousy these last few weeks, having him rolling up to the house all hours of the day, acting as though he owned you.

'I played it as cool as I could when you came back from hospital. I didn't want to rush things, but whenever I tried to talk things over and explain how I felt, you leapt away from me like a frightened horse.'

'I thought you were trying to tell me you couldn't live without Marina. That you were only staying with me because you felt guilty.'

'Christ no, that's all over, it was over that night you caught us in bed together, and threw me out. We went to Edinburgh, but it was hell, actually living with her; she got on my nerves so much I wanted to wring her neck, yacking away all the time, and never letting me think. All I could think of, actually, was you, and what a sod I'd been to you.

'Then my prodigal father turned up, and I discovered I wasn't even related to Marina, and there was no reason why I shouldn't marry her, particularly now poor old Hamish has kicked the bucket. I realized the only person in the world I wanted to be married to was you.'

'But,' I said, blushing crimson with pleasure, 'that day you all went shooting, Marina said you'd been trying to talk to me that morning to ask me for a divorce.'

'The truth was never one of Marina's strong points,' said Rory. 'She knew I was going to talk to you, we sat up half the night discussing the situation after you'd gone to bed. She said you were still crazy about Finn, and that I should let you go. I said sod that for a lark.'

He came and sat on the bed and pulled me into his arms. 'You're not still keen on him, are you? He's so pompous and self-righteous and such a bore. I was scared stiff, when you pushed off, that you'd gone to him. I borrowed Buster's plane that night and landed it in a park in Glasgow – there's been a bit of a row about that – and routed him out of his hotel bed. He was pretty angry.'

'I bet he was,' I said in awe. 'Did you really?'

'I really did,' said Rory. 'And I wonder just how much longer I am going to have to go on trying to convince you that I love you. I shouldn't think it's ever happened before in Irasa – someone falling helplessly, ludicrously in love with their own wife, after they've married them.' I felt myself blushing even more, and gazed down at my hands.

'For God's sake, Em darling, look at me.'

I picked up his hand and pressed it to my cheek.

'I've been so unhappy,' I said, 'then, in the gallery, I saw the painting you did of me. They said it was the only one you wouldn't sell.'

'I couldn't bloody well find you,' said Rory. 'I've been telephoning your mother and Nina for news every five minutes since you left.'

'Oh my God,' I said, 'I didn't ring them in case you hadn't.' I looked up and he was smiling at me and with a jolt I realized it was the first time he'd smiled without mockery; and close-up, how wan and heavy-eyed he looked, as though he hadn't slept for weeks.

'You *have* missed me,' I said in amazement. 'I really do believe you love me after all.'

'And now I'll prove it to you,' said Rory triumphantly, starting to slide down the zip of my dress.

'I'm terribly out of practice,' I muttered, suddenly shy. 'I haven't done it for ages.'

'Don't worry, it's like riding a bicycle or swimming, you never really lose the art. Get off, Walter,' he said, pushing a protesting Walter Scott on to the floor. 'This is one party you're not invited to.'

As his lips touched mine, we both began to tremble. A feeling of reckless happiness overwhelmed me. I felt his heart beating against mine and his kisses becoming more and more fierce, and the sounds of the traffic outside grew dim as they gave way to the pounding in my ears.

By the time we'd finished it was dark outside.

'God, that was lovely,' I sighed, 'we should do it more often.'

'We will,' said Rory, 'all day and all night for ever. Darling,' he said, looking suddenly worried, 'do you think you'll be able to put up with my absolutely bloody nature for the next sixty years?'

'I might,' I said, 'if you compensate from time to time with performances like the one I've just experienced.'

Rory laughed softly and rubbed the back of my neck. He lit a cigarette and lay down in the bed, pulling me into the crook of his arm.

'Rory,' I said a few minutes later, 'I know it's a terrible thing to say at a time like this, but I'm starving.'

'So am I,' he said.

'Shall we go out?'

'No, I might want you between courses, which wouldn't do in a restaurant. I'll send down for something.'

Later, as he was opening a bottle of champagne, he said, 'Darling, do you mind awfully if we don't live in Irasa any more?'

'Do I mind?' I said incredulously, 'of course I don't.'

'I'm bored with painting sheep and rocks,' he said. 'I want to paint you in the sun and give you half a dozen babies to look after to stop you having thoughts about pushing off and leaving me any more.'

'But you love Irasa.'

'It's lost its charms,' said Rory. 'I don't want you within a million miles of Finn Maclean for a start and Marina's a bloody troublemaker, and I've had enough of my mother and Buster for a few years, and lastly my new father is still there – house guestating.'

'What does he find to do all day?' I said. 'Is he still in love with Buster?'

'Yes. They're both addicted to whisky and highly-coloured reminiscences, but Alexei now seems to have other fish to fry. In the old days when Marina wanted to bug me she always used to say what she wanted was an older man. Well, Hamish was a bit too old, but Alexei looks a bit like me, and when I left he was making a marvellous job comforting her in her bereavement.'

'My goodness,' I said, staggered, 'how extraordinary. You don't mean . . . ?'

'Well, not yet. Marina fancies herself in black far too much to give it up for at least a year, but I think now that she's so rich, and Alexei is so poor, it's very much on the cards.'

'You're not jealous?' I said anxiously.

'Not at all.' He bent over and kissed me. 'But I really don't fancy Marina as a stepmother.'

THE END

Fall in love all over again with seven stories from the pen of Jilly
Cooper, 'The Jane Austen of our time' *Harpers & Queen*

EMILY
If Emily hadn't gone to Annie's party she would never have met
and married the devastating Rory Balniel.
0 552 15249 8

BELLA
Bella was the most promising young actress in London. The
dashingly handsome Ruper Henriques couldn't wait to marry her.
But Bella had a secret in her past.
0 552 15250 1

IMOGEN
Imogen's holiday on the Riviera was a revelation – and so
was she. A wild Yorkshire rose, a librarian, *and* a virgin,
she was a prize worth winning.
0 552 15254 4

PRUDENCE
Prudence was overjoyed when her boyfriend invited her
home to meet his family. But the rest of the family all
seemed to be in love with the wrong people.
0 552 15256 0

HARRIET
Harriet was shattered when a brief affair left her a penniless,
heartbroken single mother. She set off for Yorkshire to work as a
nanny to the children of eccentric scriptwriter, Cory Erskine. But
life in the country was anything but peaceful.
0 552 15251 X

OCTAVIA
When Octavia saw her school-friend's fabulous boyfriend she
knew she just had to have him. But Gareth Llewellyn
seemed determined to thwart her plans.
0 552 15252 8

LISA AND CO
Fourteen stories of great variety and undoubted class from
an author who has endeared herself to millions of
readers and bewitched them all.
0 552 15255 2

Is *your* collection complete?

CORGI BOOKS

Jilly Cooper's Rutshire Chronicles offer a heady blend of
skulduggery, sexual adventure and hilarious high jinks:

RIDERS
Takes the lid off international show jumping, a world in
which the brave horses are almost human, but the humans
frequently behave like animals.
0 552 15055 X

RIVALS
Into the cut-throat world of Corinium television comes Declan
O'Hara, a mega-star with two ravishing teenage daughters. Living
rather too closely across the valley is Rupert Campbell-Black,
divorced and as dissolute as ever.
0 552 15056 8

POLO
Follows the jet set world of the top polo players – to the *estancias*
of Argentina, to Palm Beach and Deauville, and on
to the royal polo fields of England and the glamorous
pitches of California.
0 552 15057 6

THE MAN WHO MADE HUSBANDS JEALOUS
Lysander couldn't pass a stray dog, an ill-treated horse, or a
neglected wife without rushing to the rescue. And with neglected
wives the rescue invariably led to ecstatic bonking, which didn't
please their erring husbands one bit.
0 552 15058 4

APPASSIONATA
When Abigail Rosen gets the chance to take over the Rutminster
Symphony Orchestra, she doesn't realize it is composed of the
wildest bunch of musicians ever to blow a horn or caress a fiddle
0 552 15054 1

SCORE!
Sir Robert Rannaldini, the most successful but detested conductor
in the world, had two ambitions: to seduce the ravishing Tabitha
Campbell-Black, and to put his mark on musical history by
making the definitive film of Verdi's *Don Carlos*.
0 552 15059 2

CORGI BOOKS

PANDORA
by Jilly Cooper

No picture ever came more beautiful than Raphael's *Pandora*.
Discovered by a dashing young lieutenant, Raymond Belvedon, in
a Normandy Chateau in 1944, she had cast her spell over his
family – all artists and dealers – for fifty years. Hanging in a turret
of their lovely Cotswold house, Pandora witnessed Raymond's
tempestuous wife Galena both entertaining a string of lovers, and
giving birth to her four children: Jupiter, Alizarin, Jonathan and
superbrat Sienna. Then an exquisite stranger rolls up, claiming to
be a long-lost daughter of the family, setting the three Belvedon
brothers at each other's throats. Accompanying her is her fatally
glamorous boyfriend, whose very different agenda
includes an unhealthy interest in the Raphael.

During a fireworks party, the painting is stolen. The hunt to
retrieve it takes the reader on a thrilling journey to Vienna,
Geneva, Paris, New York and London. After a nail-biting court
case and a record-smashing Old Masters sale at Sotheby's,
passionate love triumphs and *Pandora* is
restored to her rightful home.

'Open the covers of Jilly Cooper's latest novel and you lift the lid
of a Pandora's box. From the pages flies a host of delicious and
deadly vices . . . Her sheer exuberance and energy are contagious'
The Times

'This is Jilly in top form with her most sparkling novel to date'
Evening Standard

'One reads her for her joie de vivre . . . and her razor-sharp sense
of humour. Oh, and the sex' *New Statesman*

'She's irresistible . . . she frees you from the daily drudge and
deposits you in an alternative universe where love, sex and
laughter rule' *Independent on Sunday*

'The whole thing is a riot – vastly superior to anything else in a
glossy cover' *Daily Telegraph*

'A wonderful, romantic spectacular of a novel' *Spectator*

0 552 14850 4

CORGI BOOKS

CLASS
by Jilly Cooper

The English have been and always will be, obsessed by class, even though they may not realize it. And Jilly Cooper has put an accurate, acerbic, and wickedly funny finger on the idiosyncracies of the English at home, whether it be in their castles, their nice villas in Weybridge, or in their high rise council flats. In *Class* we study the peculiar habits and mores of all classes – at play, at school, at work, during courtship and marriage rituals, even the way they dress, eat, and conduct their sex lives.

Here we have Harry and Caroline Stow-Crat who love their dogs more than each other, Gideon and Samantha Upward who drink too much and are always in respectable middle-class debt, and here, too, are the wonderful Nouveau Richards, whose luxury homes are in execrable taste but blissfully comfortable with chandeliers in the loo and a bidet on every bed.

'Witheringly funny, illuminated by
astonishing brilliance'
Observer

'Enormously readable and very funny'
Cosmopolitan

0 552 14662 5

CORGI BOOKS

A LIST OF OTHER JILLY COOPER TITLES AVAILABLE FROM CORGI BOOKS AND BANTAM PRESS

15255 2	**LISA AND CO**	£6.99
15250 1	**BELLA**	£6.99
15251 X	**HARRIET**	£6.99
15254 4	**IMOGEN**	£6.99
15252 8	**OCTAVIA**	£6.99
15256 0	**PRUDENCE**	£6.99
15055 X	**RIDERS**	£6.99
15056 8	**RIVALS**	£6.99
15057 6	**POLO**	£6.99
15058 4	**THE MAN WHO MADE HUSBANDS JEALOUS**	£6.99
15054 1	**APPASSIONATA**	£6.99
15059 2	**SCORE!**	£6.99
14850 4	**PANDORA**	£6.99
14662 5	**CLASS**	£6.99
14663 3	**THE COMMON YEARS**	£5.99
99091 4	**ANIMALS IN WAR**	£6.99
04404 5	**HOW TO SURVIVE CHRISTMAS (Hardback)**	£9.99